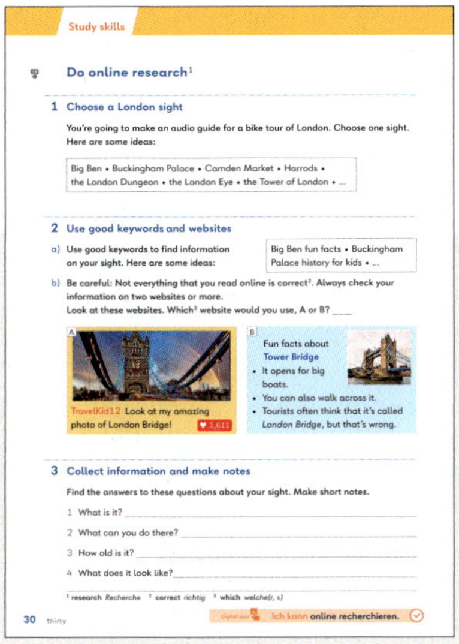
Study skills

Do online research[1]

1 Choose a London sight

You're going to make an audio guide for a bike tour of London. Choose one sight. Here are some ideas:

Big Ben • Buckingham Palace • Camden Market • Harrods • the London Dungeon • the London Eye • the Tower of London • ...

2 Use good keywords and websites

a) Use good keywords to find information on your sight. Here are some ideas:

Big Ben fun facts • Buckingham Palace history for kids • ...

b) Be careful: Not everything that you read online is correct[2]. Always check your information on two websites or more. Look at these websites. Which[3] website would you use, A or B? ___

3 Collect information and make notes

Find the answers to these questions about your sight. Make short notes.

1 What is it?
2 What can you do there?
3 How old is it?
4 What does it look like?

[1] research Recherche [2] correct richtig [3] which welche(r, s)

30 thirty — Ich kann online recherchieren.

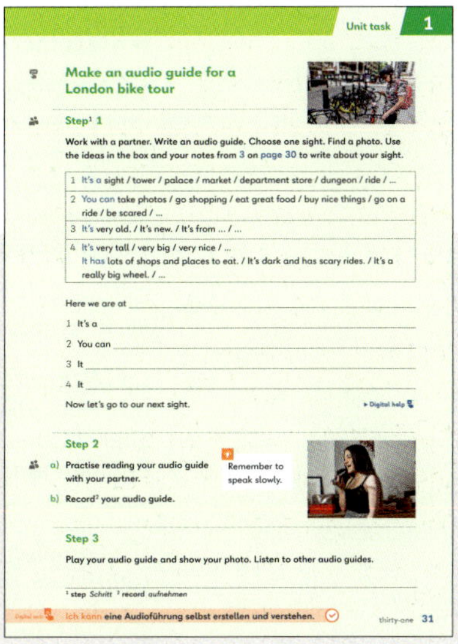
Unit task 1

Make an audio guide for a London bike tour

Step[1] 1

Work with a partner. Write an audio guide. Choose one sight. Find a photo. Use the ideas in the box and your notes from 3 on page 30 to write about your sight.

Here we are at ___

Now let's go to our next sight.

Step 2

a) Practise reading your audio guide with your partner. Remember to speak slowly.

b) Record[2] your audio guide.

Step 3

Play your audio guide and show your photo. Listen to other audio guides.

[1] step Schritt [2] record aufnehmen

Ich kann eine Audioführung selbst erstellen und verstehen. thirty-one 31

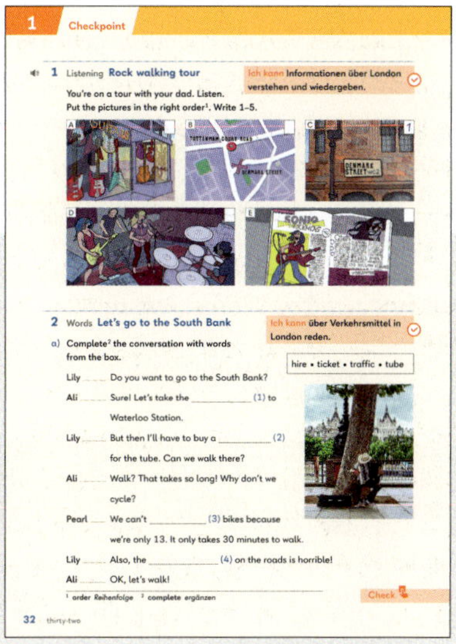
1 Checkpoint

1 Listening Rock walking tour — Ich kann Informationen über London verstehen und wiedergeben.

You're on a tour with your dad. Listen. Put the pictures in the right order[1]. Write 1–5.

2 Words Let's go to the South Bank — Ich kann über Verkehrsmittel in London reden.

a) Complete[2] the conversation with words from the box.

hire • ticket • traffic • tube

[1] order Reihenfolge [2] complete ergänzen

32 thirty-two

***Study skills***

Hier übst du wichtige Lerntechniken.

***Unit task***

In der *Unit task* erstellst du ein größeres Produkt, z.B. eine Präsentation.

***Checkpoint***

Hier überprüfst du, wie gut du gelernt hast.

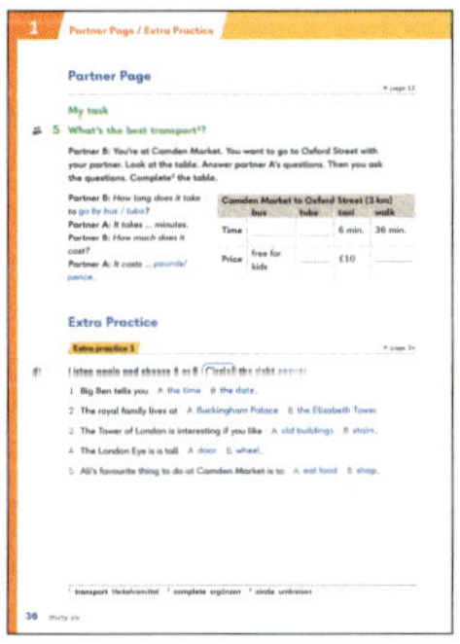

***Extra practice***

Am Ende jeder Unit findest du noch mehr Übungen.

**Vokabelliste**

Am Ende jeder Unit gibt es eine Liste mit den neuen Vokabeln.

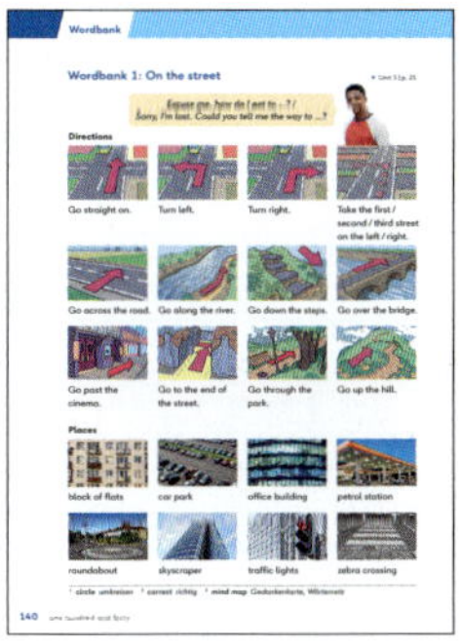

***Wordbanks***

Du hast neue Themen kennengelernt. Nach den Units findest du weitere Wörter dazu.

# lighthouse 3

Lern- und Arbeitsheft für Lernende mit erhöhtem Förderbedarf

*Im Auftrag des Verlages herausgegeben von*
Ulrike Rath, Aachen
*sowie*
Martin Bastkowski, Schellerten;
Sonja Mahne, Basel;
Berit Schaarschmidt, Aschaffenburg

*Erarbeitet von*
Olivia Wintgens, Würselen; Rebecca Robb Benne, Kopenhagen; Zoe Thorne, Royston
*sowie*
Jennifer O'Hagan, Bristol und Chris Maxwell, Berlin (*Checkpoints*)

*In Zusammenarbeit mit der Englischredaktion*
Klaus Unger (Projektleitung), Sandhya Gupta, Karin Wedepohl, *sowie* Georg Raspe, Düsseldorf (*Vocabulary*)

*Beratende Mitwirkung*
Stella Halank, Berlin; Lina Hein-Gehrmann, Wuppertal

*Medienmanagement*
Silke Kirchhoff

*Illustrationen*
Harald Ardeias, Schelklingen; Irina Zinner, Hamburg

*Fotos*
Chocolate Films, London

*Umschlaggestaltung*
Rosendahl, Berlin

*Layoutkonzept*
Klein & Halm, Berlin

*Layout und technische Umsetzung*
Klein & Halm, Berlin

**www.cornelsen.de**



1. Auflage, 1. Druck 2024

Alle Drucke dieser Auflage sind inhaltlich unverändert und können im Unterricht nebeneinander verwendet werden.

ISBN 9783060346158 (Ausgabe für Lernende)
ISBN 9783060346165 (Ausgabe für Lehrkräfte)

Produktnummer 1100030004 E-Book

Druck: AZ Druck und Datentechnik GmbH, Kempten

PEFC
PEFC/04-31-2260

PEFC-zertifiziert
Dieses Produkt stammt aus nachhaltig bewirtschafteten Wäldern und kontrollierten Quellen
www.pefc.de

# lighthouse 3

## Lern- und Arbeitsheft

Audios online verfügbar unter
go.cornelsen.de    **Code:** wekidu

Dein Arbeitsheft findest du auch in der **Cornelsen Lernen App**.
Siehst du eines dieser Symbole in deinem Arbeitsheft, findest du in der App …

- alle **Audios**
- alle **Videos** und **Erklärfilme**
- **Quizfragen, Hilfen** und **Lösungen** zu ausgewählten Aufgaben

Cornelsen

# Inhalt

## Hello! **Where we're from**

# Unit 1 **London: City life**

Wenn du die Seiten bearbeitet hast, setze ein Häkchen in die Box.

| | | | Seite |
|---|---|---|---|
| London: City life | Ich kann Informationen über London verstehen und wiedergeben.<br>This big sight at the Houses of Parliament is very famous. |  | 14–15 ☐ |
| Topic 1 | Ich kann über Verkehrsmittel in London reden.<br>The underground, also called "the tube", is a great way to travel in London. |   | 16–17 ☐ |
| Topic 2 | Ich kann eine Tour planen.<br>Ride your own Segway. |  | 18–21 ☐ |
| Topic 3 | Ich kann das Leben in der Großstadt und in meiner Gegend beschreiben.<br>London is my city and it's always busy. |  | 22–25 ☐ |
| Story | Ich kann einer Geschichte folgen und sie diskutieren.<br>First they went ... Then ...<br>The story was exciting ... |  | 26–28 ☐ |
| Viewing | Ich kann über Hilfe für andere sprechen.<br>I want to help neighbours with chores. |  | 29 ☐ |
| Study skills | Ich kann online recherchieren.<br>Be careful: Not everything that you read online is correct. |  | 30 ☐ |
| Unit task | Ich kann eine Audioführung erstellen und verstehen.<br>Here we are at Buckingham Palace. |  | 31 ☐ |

## Unit 2 **Manchester: Who we are**

Wenn du die Seiten bearbeitet hast, setze ein Häkchen in die Box.

# Unit 3 **Scotland: Adventure**

Wenn du die Seiten bearbeitet hast, setze ein Häkchen in die Box.

| | | | Seite |
|---|---|---|---|
| **Scotland: Adventure** | **Ich kann über Schottland reden.**<br>I think visiting Eilean Donan Castle looks ... |  | 72–73 ☐ |
| **Topic 1** | **Ich kann Geschichten und Legenden verstehen.**<br>In my opinion, Nessie is just a story for tourists because ... |  | 74–77 ☐ |
| **Topic 2** | **Ich kann über Aktivitäten und Abenteuer reden.**<br>I know a scary film. It's called ... |  | 78–81 ☐ |
| **Topic 3** | **Ich kann über die Natur sprechen.**<br>Nature is important because ... |  | 82–83 ☐ |
| **Story** | **Ich kann Entscheidungen in einer Geschichte besprechen.**<br>Next time, Grace should ... |  | 84–86 ☐ |
| **Viewing** | **Ich kann über Unternehmungen in Schottland sprechen.**<br>On the Isle of Skye, they don't ... |  | 87 ☐ |
| **Study skills** | **Ich kann Ideen für eine Geschichte ordnen.**<br>Who? Where? When? What? |  | 88 ☐ |
| **Unit task** | **Ich kann eine kurze Abenteuergeschichte schreiben.**<br>Last year my dad and I went to Hamburg. | 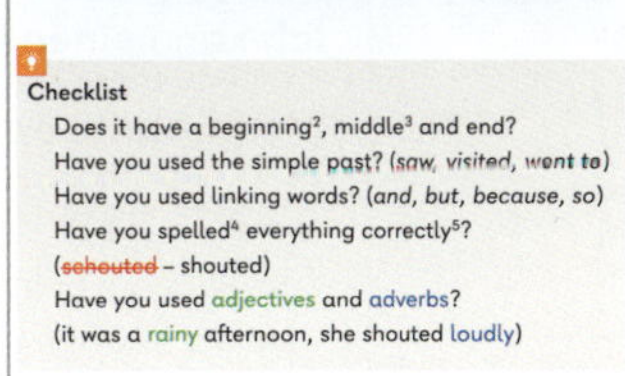<br>Checklist<br>Does it have a beginning[2], middle[3] and end?<br>Have you used the simple past? (saw, visited, went to)<br>Have you used linking words? (and, but, because, so)<br>Have you spelled[4] everything correctly[5]?<br>(~~schouted~~ – shouted)<br>Have you used adjectives and adverbs?<br>(it was a rainy afternoon, she shouted loudly) | 89 ☐ |

## Unit 4 **Wales: Digital life**

Wenn du die Seiten bearbeitet hast, setze ein Häkchen in die Box.

# Unit 5 **Two Irelands: Together**

OPTIONAL

Wenn du die Seiten bearbeitet hast, setze ein Häkchen in die Box.

| | | | Seite |
|---|---|---|---|
| **Two Irelands: Together** | **Ich kann über Irland und Nordirland sprechen.**<br>I want to go to the Titantic Belfast museum. |  | 130–131<br>☐ |
| **Topic 1** | **Ich kann eine Reise planen und darüber reden.**<br>How much is it?<br>Does the room have its own bathroom?<br>Is there a hot breakfast? |  | 132–133<br>☐ |
| **Viewing** | **Ich kann über Ängste und Mut sprechen.**<br>When Tina dances with her class at the end, she feels ... |  | 134<br>☐ |

# Hello!
# Where we're from

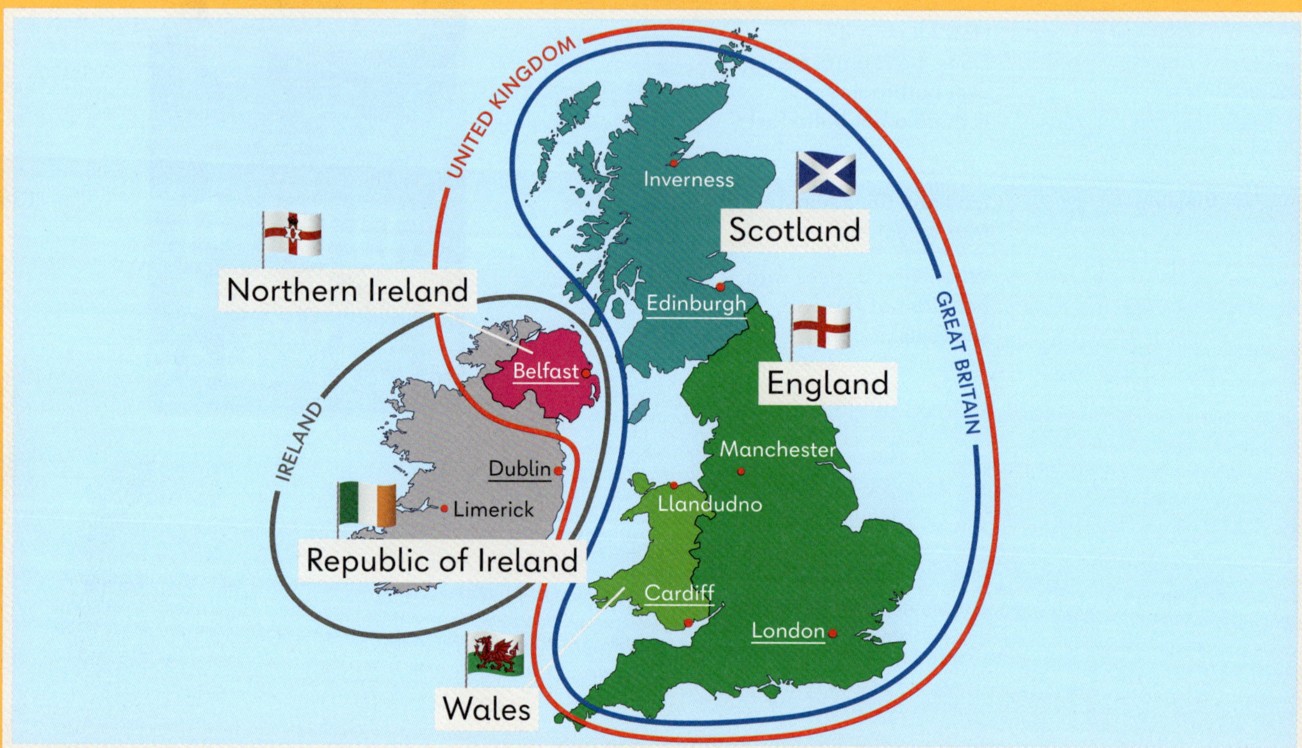


## 1 Viewing **The United Kingdom and Ireland**

a) Before you watch **Look at the map. Draw lines[1]. What countries make up …**

| | |
|---|---|
| 1 Great Britain (GB)? | England, Wales, Scotland, Northern Ireland |
| 2 the island of Ireland? | England, Wales, Scotland |
| 3 the United Kingdom (UK)? | The Republic of Ireland, Northern Ireland |

b) **Watch the video and check.**

[1] line *Linie*

## 2 Speaking **Hello!**

a) **Listen and read what the students say.**

b) **Where are they from? Point to[1] the places on the map on** **page 10****. Check with your partner.**

*London is here on the map.*

c) **Three greetings[2] on this page are not in English. Find and circle[3] them.**

**Good to know**

In Schottland sprechen manche Menschen Schottisch-Gälisch, in Wales Walisisch und in Irland Irisch-Gälisch.

[1] **point to** *zeigen auf* [2] **greeting** *Begrüßung* [3] **circle** *umkreisen*

A This place has it all.

B A musician playing the bagpipes

C Amazing modern buildings

## 3 Listening **Where we live**

a) Before you listen **Look at the photos (A–F). What can you see?**

*In photo A, I can see ...*

b) **Listen to the six students and match[1] them to the photos. Write A–F in the boxes.**

1 Pearl C

2 Omar

3 Grace

4 Dylan

5 Jack

6 Orla

[1] **match** *zuordnen*

D

Street art everywhere

E

Conwy Castle

F

Boats in a city

## 4 The best place

What can you say about the photos? Write two sentences[1]. Then talk to your partner.

| | | |
|---|---|---|
| I think that | photo A/B/ ... looks | amazing • funny • interesting • nice • boring • ... |
| I like | big cities • boat trips • castles • history • music • street art • ... | |

[1] **sentence** *Satz*

Digital quiz

Ich kann über das Vereinigte Königreich und Irland sprechen.

# Unit 1
# London: City life[1]

Go shopping and eat amazing food.

This big sight at the Houses of Parliament is very famous.

**1** Listening **Your London, my London**

**Lily is in London. She's talking to her new friend Ali.**

a) Before you listen **Match[2] the sights to the photos. Write 1–5 on the right photo.**

| |
|---|
| 1 Big Ben • 2 Buckingham Palace • 3 Camden Market • 4 The London Eye • 5 The Tower of London |

b) **Listen. Where are Ali and Lily going this weekend? Circle[3] the sight.**

1 The London Eye     2 Camden Market     3 Tower of London

▸ Extra practice 1, p. 36

[1] **life** *Leben*  [2] **match** *zuordnen*  [3] **circle** *umkreisen*

**Nach dieser Unit kann ich ...**

- ◯ Informationen über London verstehen und wiedergeben
- ◯ über Verkehrsmittel in London reden
- ◯ eine Tour planen
- ◯ das Leben in der Großstadt und in meiner Gegend beschreiben
- ◯ online recherchieren

**Unit task**

- ◯ einen Audioguide für London erstellen

C

The royal family lives in this famous palace.

D

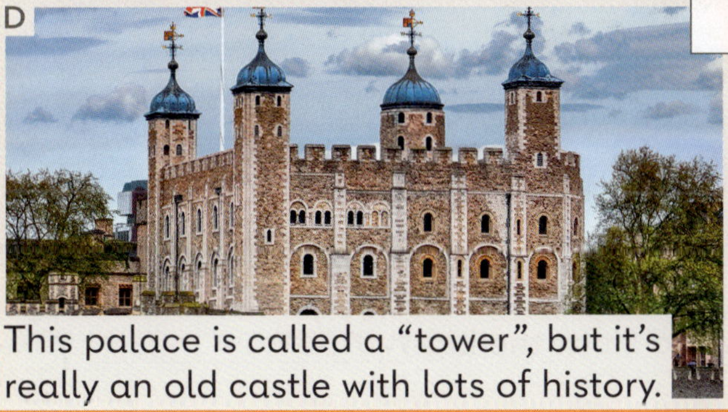

This palace is called a "tower", but it's really an old castle with lots of history.

E

This wheel is called an "eye". You can take great photos on it!

## 2 Speaking **Visiting London**

**What can you say about the places in 1? Tell each other.**

| | | | |
|---|---|---|---|
| I think that | Big Ben • Buckingham Palace • Camden Market • the London Eye • the Tower of London | looks | cool • interesting fun • exciting • ... |
| I like to | take photos • see famous sights • go to old castles • go shopping • eat amazing food • ... | | |

Digital quiz

**Ich kann Informationen über London verstehen und wiedergeben.**

# Travelling in London

## 1 Reading London's public transport

a) Before you read **How can you travel in big cities? Tell a partner.**

You can go by ...

car • train • ...

b) **Read the text. Then complete[1] 1–4 with one word.**

**No car? No problem!**

You don't need a car in London! The underground, also called "the tube", is a great way to travel in London. Or try London's famous red buses. Go up the stairs and sit at the big windows at the front – it's fun!
You can also hire bikes all over London with different apps. There's a lot of traffic, so be careful. Wear a helmet if you can.
Walking is a great way to see London! But remember that people drive on the left in the UK. Before you cross the road, look right first!

1 On the bus, it's fun to go up the stairs and sit at the big windows ______.

2 "The tube" is the name for the ______.

3 When you cycle in London, it's a good idea to wear a ______.

4 If you're walking across the road, remember that you first look ______.

## 2 Words Transport

**Match[2].**

| | |
|---|---|
| 1 buy | a the tube / bus / train |
| 2 cross | b bikes |
| 3 take | c a ticket |
| 4 hire | d the road |

▶ Extra practice 2–3, p. 37

[1] **complete** *ergänzen* [2] **match** *zuordnen*

## 3 Listening A trip

a) Listen to Lily, Ali and Pearl. How will they get to Camden Market? Circle[1] the right answer.

1 They will go by tube. 2 They will walk.

b) Listen again. True (T) or false[2] (F)?

1 There's only one way to get there. F

2 It takes 25 minutes to walk. ☐

3 A ticket for the tube costs £1.60. ☐

4 Lily wants to go by bus. ☐

## 4 On the way[3]

Use the will-future: *'ll* or *won't*.

Ali — You *'ll* ______ (1) love the market, Lily.

Lily — I don't have a lot of money, so I ______ (2) buy much. I ______ (3) just look at the shops.

**Remember**

Du verwendest das *will-future* um zu sagen, was wahrscheinlich in der Zukunft geschehen wird (*I'll = I will*).
Du verwendest *won't* (= *will not*) um zu sagen, was nicht geschehen wird.

▸ Extra practice 4–5, p. 38

**My task**

## 5 What's the best transport[4]?

You're at Camden Market. You want to go to Oxford Street. Partner A: Complete the table. Ask and answer questions. Partner B: Look at page 36.

**Partner A:** *How long does it take to walk / go by taxi?*
**Partner B:** *It takes ... minutes.*
**Partner A:** *How much does it cost?*
**Partner B:** *It costs ... pounds / pence.*

| Camden Market to Oxford Street (3 km) | bus | tube | taxi | walk |
|---|---|---|---|---|
| Time | 17 min. | 7 min. | ______ | ______ |
| Price | ______ ______ | 90p | ______ | free |

[1] circle *umkreisen* [2] false *falsch* [3] on the way *auf dem Weg* [4] transport *Verkehrsmittel*

Digital quiz — Ich kann über Verkehrsmittel in London reden.

# A different kind of tour

## 1 Reading **Which[1] tour?**

a) Before you read **Pearl wants to go on a tour. Look at the tours 1–3 and the photos A–C. Write the correct[2] tour number in the box.**

1 Ghost Bus Tour    2 London Segway Tour    3 Rock Walking Tour

A  ☐

Calling all music fans! Go on our Rock Walking Tour to see important places of music history. You'll visit Denmark Street, where many rock bands and singers made their albums. We'll go to the best music shops too. Then we'll have lunch at Hard Rock Cafe!

**WEEKENDS ONLY**

B  ☐

If you're scared of the dark, you won't like this tour! Take our Ghost Bus for a tour of the scariest places in London. Will you see ghosts in the Tower of London? Can you go into the London Dungeon?
Let's find out ...

**MEET US EVERY DAY AT 9 P. M. AT THE GHOST BUS STOP**

C  ☐

See the most important London sights! Ride your own Segway. We'll show you Buckingham Palace, where the royal family live. Cross the River Thames on the beautiful Tower Bridge. And visit the home of the prime minister at 10 Downing Street!

**2 P. M. EVERY DAY EXCEPT MONDAYS**

b) **Read about the tours. Then read the sentences[3]. Choose tour A, B or C.**

1 This tour is in the evening. B
2 You can buy something on this tour. ☐
3 You can see famous homes on this tour. ☐
4 This tour is only on Saturdays and Sundays. ☐
5 You must be brave to do this tour. ☐
6 You can eat on this tour. ☐

 c) **Tell your partner which tour you want to do. Then circle it.**

| I want to do the | Ghost Bus Tour • London Segway Tour • Rock Walking Tour |
|---|---|

▸ Extra practice 6, p. 39

[1] **which** *welche(r, s)*  [2] **correct** *korrekt*  [3] **sentence** *Satz*

Erklär-film

## 2 Looking at language **Conditional sentences type 1 (If-clause, type 1)**

**Read sentences 1 and 2. Then read the rule in the box and (circle) the correct answer A or B.**

1 "If you look to your left, you'll see the most beautiful building in London."
2 "If the King is at home today, there'll be a flag on the building."

Mit dem *if-Satz, Typ 1 (conditional sentence, type 1)* sagst du, was unter bestimmten Bedingungen geschehen wird. *If*-Sätze bestehen aus zwei Teilen:

- einer Voraussetzung (*if*-Satz im *simple present*) und
- der Folge (Hauptsatz im *will-future*).

Beispiel: If the King is at home today, there'll be a flag on the building.

1 If the King is ... beschreibt A die Folge B die Voraussetzung.
2 there'll be ... beschreibt A die Folge B die Voraussetzung.

## 3 What will we do if ...?

**Pearl is planning activities for after the tour. Draw lines[1].**

| | | | |
|---|---|---|---|
| 1 | If Aunt Vera sees a famous person, | A | they'll buy too many toys. |
| 2 | If it is rainy, | B | he'll want to stop and eat. |
| 3 | If my cousins go to Hamleys toy shop, | C | we won't stay outside. |
| 4 | If Uncle Roy sees good food, | D | she'll be so happy! |

## 4 Pearl's family's visit

**Complete[2] the if-sentences. Use the simple present.**

1 If Pearl's cousins *are* (be) late, they won't get the train.

2 If they ________ (see) some musicians on the street, they'll listen to the music.

3 If Aunt Vera ________ (find) a nice book, she'll buy it.

4 If Uncle Roy ________ (leave) his hat on the bus, he won't be happy!

▸ Extra practice 7, p. 40

[1] **line** *Linie* [2] **complete** *ergänzen*

## 5 Speaking **Quiz-quiz-swap**

**What will you do if you go to London? Complete the sentences. Tell your partner.**

*If I go to London, …*

I'll eat ______________________ . | burgers • pizza • fish and chips • kebab • …

I'll travel by ______________________ . | bus • underground • bike • …

I'll visit ______________________ . | Big Ben • the London Eye • …

## 6 Mediation **St James's Park**

**Good to know**

London has lots of parks.

**You're on a walking tour in St James's Park. A German tourist needs your help. Write your answers in German.**

**Guide** This is St James's Park. It's not the biggest park in London, but I think it's the most beautiful.

**Tourist** Was hat er gerade über den Park gesagt?

**You** St James's Park ist *nicht der größte Park, aber* ______________________ .

**Guide** The biggest park in London is Hyde Park.

**Tourist** Was hat er zum Hyde Park gesagt?

**You** Der Hyde Park ist ______________________ .

**Guide** Now, if you look over the Blue Bridge, you'll see Buckingham Palace. And the other way, you'll see the London Eye.

**Tourist** Was hat er über die Gebäude gesagt?

**You** Dort ______________________ .

**Guide** Look! We're very lucky to see those birds[1]! Aren't they beautiful?

**You** ______________________

[1] **bird** *Vogel*

## 7 Viewing **A virtual[1] tour of London**

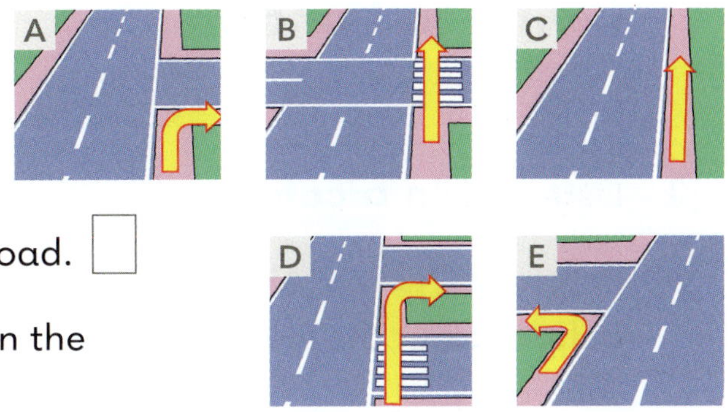


a) Before you watch **Match[2] the pictures A–E to the directions[3].**

1 Go straight on. C
2 Turn left. ☐
3 Turn right. ☐
4 Go across the road. ☐
5 Take the road on the right. ☐

b) Viewing **Complete the directions with the words in the box. Then watch the video and check.**

| across • left<br>right • straight |
|---|

1 Let's go ____________ (1) the roundabout[4] and go straight over the road.
2 Let's take the third[5] street on the ____________ (2).
3 Turn ____________ (3) at the river and go ____________ (4) on.

## My task

## 8 A tour of London

**Write the directions from Buckingham Palace to the London Eye in your exercise book. Use the ideas in the box.**

▸ Digital help

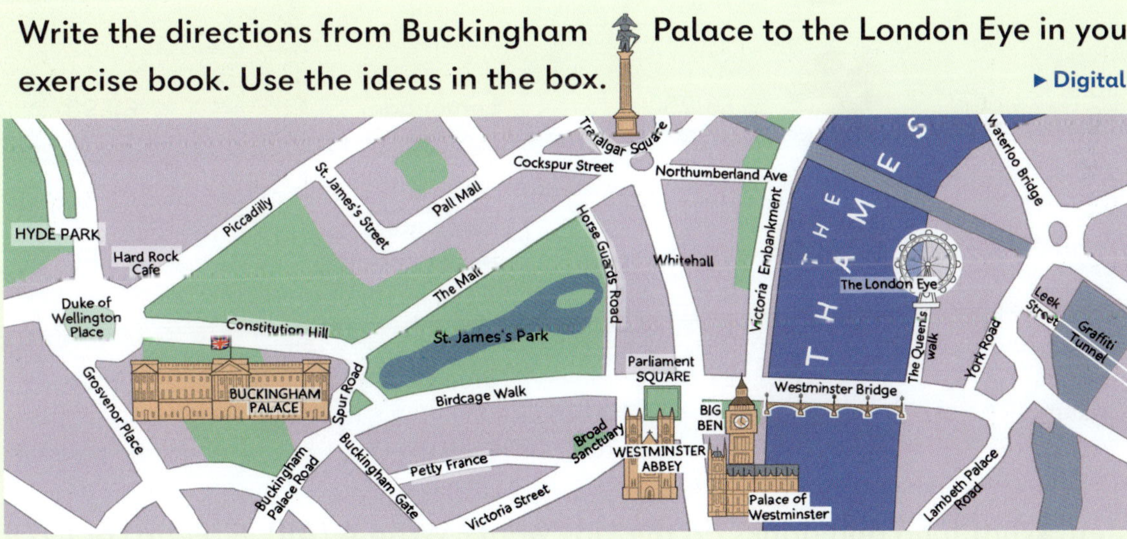


*Start at Buckingham Palace. Then go straight on ...*

▸ Wordbank 1, p. 140

| | |
|---|---|
| Go straight on ... | The Mall • The Queen's Walk |
| Turn left / right at ... | Trafalgar Square • Westminster Bridge |
| Go across ... | Westminster Bridge • the road |
| Now stop. You have arrived! You're at ... | |

[1] **virtual** *virtuell* [2] **match** *zuordnen* [3] **direction** *Wegbeschreibung* [4] **roundabout** *Kreisverkehr*
[5] **third** *dritte/dritter/drittes*

Digital quiz **Ich kann eine Tour planen.**

# Living in London

## 1 Listening **In a cafe**

a) Before you listen **Ali, Pearl and Lily are at a Lebanese[1] cafe. Look at the menu. What dishes do you know? Tell your partner.**

*I know ...*

**Menu**

| **Small dishes** | | | | **Drinks** | | | |
|---|---|---|---|---|---|---|---|
| Hummus (chickpea dip) |  | £5.75 | | Apple juice | | £2.50 | |
| Halloumi cheese with cucumber and tomatoes |  | £6.25 | L | Orange juice | | £2.50 | |
| Spicy sausages with lemon |  | £6.50 | | Cola | | £2.50 | |
| Falafel with sauce |  | £6.25 | | Lemonade | | £2.95 | |
| Spicy potatoes |  | £6.50 | | Bottomless tea or coffee | | £2.50 | |
| Chicken and potatoes with lemon |  | £7.50 | | Bread |  | 90 p | |

b) **Listen. What food and drinks do the kids want? Write A (Ali), P (Pearl) or L (Lily) in the menu next to their food and drinks.**

c) **Complete[3] 1–4. Use the words in the box. Then listen again and check.**

| I'll • like • please • some |
|---|

1 Could I have ________ tea, please?

2 I'd ______ a cola, please.

3 ________ have the falafel, please.

4 Could we have some bread too, ________?

[1] **Lebanese** *libanesisch* [2] **menu** *Speisekarte* [3] **complete** *ergänzen*

## 2 Word building **Everything looks wonderful!**

**The waiter has come with the food. Read. Then circle[1] A or B.**

1 *Wonderful* bedeutet A wundervoll B furchtbar.

2 *Careful* bedeutet A vorsichtig B unvorsichtig.

3 *Careless* bedeutet A vorsichtig B unvorsichtig.

4 *Bottomless* bedeutet A übervoll B ohne Boden, d. h. du kannst so viel trinken, wie du möchtest.

Die Endung *-ful* bedeutet „voll von", *-less* bedeutet „ohne".
Damit kannst du viele Wörter erschließen.

## 3 Speaking **Let's order!**

a) **Who says what? Read and write W (waitress) or C (customer[2]) next to 1–4.**

1 *I'll have / I'd like ..., please.* ☐

2 *Could I have ..., please?* ☐

3 *Would you like anything else?* ☐

4 *What would you like to drink / eat?* ☐

b) Role-play **Make a group of three. One student is the waitress or waiter, and the others are the customers. Talk to each other. Use the phrases[3] in a).**

[1] **circle** *umkreisen* [2] **customer** *Kunde, Kundin* [3] **phrase** *Ausdruck*

## 4 Song My London

**Pearl takes Ali and Lily to Rap Club to listen to some music.**

a) Before you listen **What's good or bad about a big city like London? Look at the ideas on the right and complete the table.**

*crowds, graffiti, noise, public transport, smells, sport teams ...*

| 👍 | 👎 |
| --- | --- |
| *good things to eat* | *traffic* |
| | |
| | |

b) **Listen to the song and read the text. Does the singer like London? Circle A or B.**

A Yes B No

**My London** ♫

*My London, it's not about the Tower or the Dungeon*
*or the big wheel – my London's real, it's something that you feel.*
*It's here I was born, with all the traffic and the car horns.*
*Capital L, with all the noises and the smells*
*and Big Ben's bell goes bong, can't stay away too long.*
*Don't get me wrong, we are strong, that's why I wrote this song.*

*My London – sing it loud, I'm so proud.*
*My London – I don't care about the crowds or the grey clouds.*
*My London, my London!*

*London is my city and it's always pretty busy.*
*On the walls we have graffiti and the city's never sleepy.*
*We have to help the homeless, I know this.*
*Yeah, we have people on the street,*
*but we also have hip-hop beats and good things to eat.*
*I know it's not perfect,*
*but it's my favourite place on earth, it's worth it.*

*My London ...*

**horn** *Hupe*
**capital** *Großbuchstabe*
**bell** *Glocke*
**I don't care** *es ist mir egal*
**cloud** *Wolke*
**pretty busy** *ziemlich hektisch*
**sleepy** *schläfrig*
**worth** *wert*

c) **Listen to the song again. Can you rap it too?**

## 5 Global goals **Green cities**

**'Green cities' is one global goal[1] to make the world a better place.**

a) Listening **Lily and her friends talk at Rap Club. Listen and circle A or B.**

Before Lily moved to London, she thought it was … A boring. B loud and dirty.

b) **What do you find in green cities? Tick[2] (✓). Then listen again and check.**

1 traffic, rubbish ☐
2 trees, parks ☐
3 bike lanes, public transport ☐
4 clothes swaps ☐

## My task

## 6 A blog post about city life

a) **Read the post. Does Baz like city life? Circle:** A Yes B No

www.example.com/city-life

**My life in the city by Baz**
In my opinion, city life is amazing. There are lots of activities and interesting places in my city. You can eat great food. I love my sport teams – game days are the best! Sometimes it's very noisy. I don't like that! I don't like villages in the country very much. I think they're boring!

b) **Do you like big cities? Write a post in your exercise book. You can use these ideas.**

▸ Digital help ▸ Wordbank 2, p. 141

| | | |
|---|---|---|
| I think / In my opinion … | city life is | amazing / OK / horrible / … |
| There are … | too many people / lots of friendly people / … | |
| You can / You can't … | go cycling / play outside / do fun things / … | |
| I like / I love … | my | sport teams / youth centre / neighbours / … |
| Sometimes … | it's very | busy / loud / … |
| I like / I don't like | villages / small towns / big cities. | |

c) **Put the posts on the wall. Read the posts. Give feedback.**

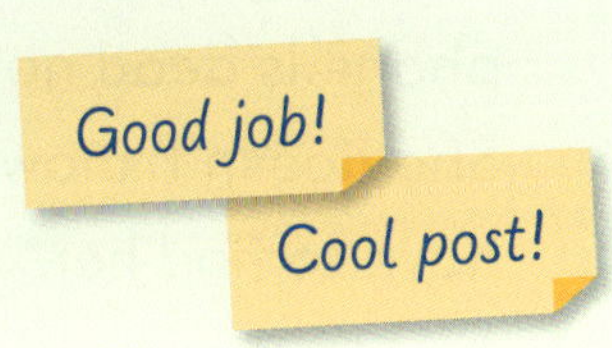


[1] **global goal** *weltweites Ziel* [2] **tick** *abhaken*

Digital quiz Ich kann das Leben in einer Stadt und meiner Gegend beschreiben.

# Where is Lily?

## 1 Before you read **Places in London**

**Look at the photos on** pages 26–27**. Find them on the map.**

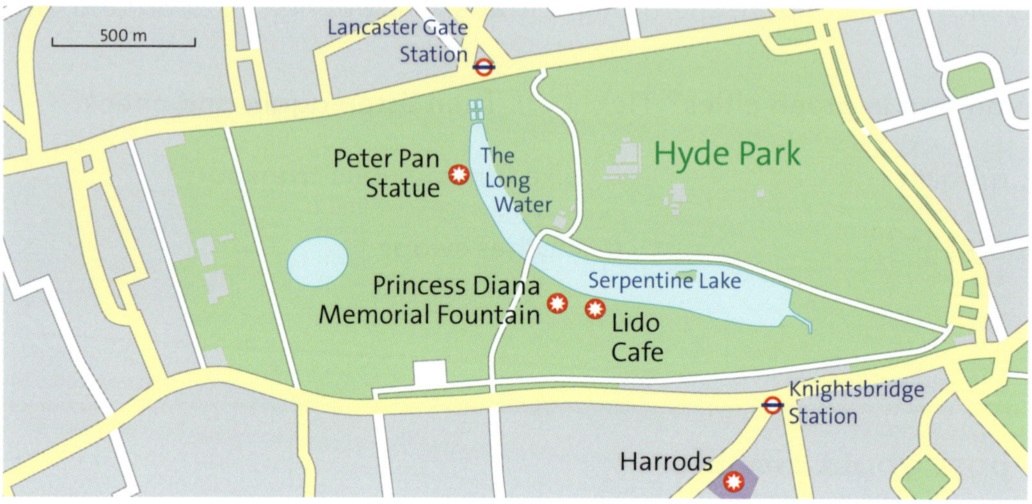


## 2 Reading **Let's find Lily**

**Read the story and follow Ali and Pearl on the map in 1.**

Pearl looked at Ali. 'That was Lily's dad on the phone. She didn't come home after school, and she isn't answering her phone. Her dad asked if she was with us.'

'Hmm,' said Ali. 'She sent me some photos from Harrods right after school.'

'Harrods? The department store? Why was she there?' asked Pearl.

'She wanted to buy some special chocolates for her mum's birthday. Look!' said Ali.

'Yeah[1], good photos! So maybe her phone is dead now? Or maybe she's lost. She doesn't know London very well. We have to find her.'

*Harrods* ✓

[1] **yeah** *ja*

Pearl and Ali took the tube to Knightsbridge and walked to Harrods.

'If we ask the doorkeeper, maybe he'll help us,' said Pearl.
She showed the doorkeeper a photo of Lily on her phone.
'Excuse me? Was this girl here?'

The doorkeeper looked at the photo.
'Yes, she was. When she came out, she asked me for directions to Hyde Park.'

Pearl and Ali walked to Hyde Park. They asked at the Lido about Lily.

Lido Cafe

'No sorry,' said the woman at the desk. 'I haven't seen her.'

Suddenly Pearl saw something.
'Those red sunglasses over there – they're Lily's! So she *was* here.
But where is she now?
Oh no, I hope she's OK.'

Suddenly Pearl remembered something.
'Look, here's Princess Diana's Memorial Fountain. Lily's mum loves Princess Diana. Maybe Lily wanted to take photos of the fountain for her mum.
Let's ask people.'

Princess Diana Memorial Fountain

'Yes, I remember her,' said a woman.
'She asked me the way to the nearest tube station, so I gave her directions to Lancaster Gate. It's easy, just follow The Long Water that way until you come to a big road.'

Pearl and Ali said thank you and started to run.
'If we're fast, we'll find her at the tube station!' said Ali.
The kids were fast, but when they got to the Peter Pan Statue, Pearl stopped.
'This is too hard,' she said. 'Run to the station alone. I'll come after you.'

Peter Pan Statue

## 3 The route[1]

a) **Read Ali and Pearl's route to find Lily. Put the letters in the right order[2].**

1 First they went to (Hrosdar) H _a_ _r_ _r_ _o_ _d_ s.

2 Then they went to the (Loid) L ___ ___ o in Hyde Park.

3 After that, they checked the (fonutina) f ___ ___ ___ ___ ___ ___ n in Hyde Park.

b) Listening **Listen to the end of the story. What happened? (Circle[3]) the right words.**

In the end, Pearl / Ali found Lily at the station / statue.

## 4 Why?

a) **Read the story again and match[4] the sentence[5] parts.**

| | |
|---|---|
| 1 Lily's dad called Pearl because | A they wanted to meet Lily at the station. |
| 2 Pearl and Ali wanted to find Lily because | B Lily didn't come home after school. |
| 3 Ali and Pearl started to run because | C she couldn't run any more. |
| 4 Pearl stopped at the statue because | D she didn't know London very well. |

b) Listening **Listen to the end of the story again and match the correct sentence parts.**

| | |
|---|---|
| 1 Lily can't call or text her dad because | A her dad will be worried and she wanted to get home quickly. |
| 2 Lily wants to get the train because | B her phone is dead. |

▶ Extra practice 8, p. 40

## 5 What do you think?

**Did you like the story? (Circle). Then talk to your partner.**

*The story was ...* | exciting • interesting • Ok • boring

[1] **route** *Route* [2] **order** *Reihenfolge* [3] **circle** *umkreisen* [4] **match** *zuordnen* [5] **sentence** *Satz*



Digital quiz **Ich kann einer Geschichte folgen und sie diskutieren.**

# On the streets of London

## 1 Before you watch **What does it mean[1]?**

Match[2].

| | | | |
|---|---|---|---|
| 1 | A homeless person doesn't | A | work for free. |
| 2 | A community is | B | have a home. |
| 3 | To make a difference[3] means to | C | make the world better. |
| 4 | To volunteer[4] means to | D | a group of people. |

## 2 Viewing **Josh and Jade**

a) Look at the notes about Josh and Jade. Watch the video. Circle[5] the right answers.

A
Name: Josh / Jade
Job: vet / hairdresser
She finds / helps homeless people's dogs.

B
Name: Josh / Jade
Job: vet / hairdresser
He cuts / cleans homeless people's hair.

b) Watch the video again. Are the sentences true (T) or false[6] (F)?

1 Josh got the idea to volunteer from one of Jade's posts. ☐

2 Even if you don't have money, you can make people smile. ☐

3 Josh feels happiest when he volunteers. ☐

## 3 Life skills **Make a difference!**

How can you make a difference? Read the ideas. Say which[7] one you want to do.

*I want to ...*

do a clean-up day • help neighbours with chores • volunteer at a charity • give things to a charity shop

[1] **mean** *bedeuten* [2] **match** *zuordnen* [3] **make a difference** *etwas bewirken*
[4] **volunteer** *freiwillig arbeiten* [5] **circle** *umkreisen* [6] **false** *falsch* [7] **which** *welche(r, s)*

# Do online research[1]

## 1 Choose a London sight

You're going to make an audio guide for a bike tour of London. Choose one sight. Here are some ideas:

Big Ben • Buckingham Palace • Camden Market • Harrods • the London Dungeon • the London Eye • the Tower of London • ...

## 2 Use good keywords and websites

a) Use good keywords to find information on your sight. Here are some ideas:

Big Ben fun facts • Buckingham Palace history for kids • ...

b) Be careful: Not everything that you read online is correct[2]. Always check your information on two websites or more.
Look at these websites. Which[3] website would you use, A or B? ____

A

TravelKid12 Look at my amazing photo of London Bridge! ♥ 1,611

B

Fun facts about **Tower Bridge**

- It opens for big boats.
- You can also walk across it.
- Tourists often think that it's called *London Bridge*, but that's wrong.

## 3 Collect information and make notes

Find the answers to these questions about your sight. Make short notes.

1 What is it? ____________________

2 What can you do there? ____________________

3 How old is it? ____________________

4 What does it look like? ____________________

[1] **research** *Recherche* [2] **correct** *richtig* [3] **which** *welche(r, s)*

Digital quiz **Ich kann online recherchieren.**

# Make an audio guide for a London bike tour

## Step[1] 1

Work with a partner. Write an audio guide. Choose one sight. Find a photo. Use the ideas in the box and your notes from 3 on page 30 to write about your sight.

| | |
|---|---|
| 1 | It's a sight / tower / palace / market / department store / dungeon / ride / ... |
| 2 | You can take photos / go shopping / eat great food / buy nice things / go on a ride / be scared / ... |
| 3 | It's very old. / It's new. / It's from ... / ... |
| 4 | It's very tall / very big / very nice / ... It has lots of shops and places to eat. / It's dark and has scary rides. / It's a really big wheel. / ... |

Here we are at ______________________________.

1 It's a ______________________________.

2 You can ______________________________.

3 It ______________________________.

4 It ______________________________.

Now let's go to our next sight.

▸ Digital help

## Step 2

a) Practise reading your audio guide with your partner.

b) Record[2] your audio guide.

Remember to speak slowly.

## Step 3

Play your audio guide and show your photo. Listen to other audio guides.

[1] step *Schritt* [2] record *aufnehmen*

Digital quiz

Ich kann eine Audioführung selbst erstellen und verstehen.

## 1 Listening **Rock walking tour**

**Ich kann Informationen über London verstehen und wiedergeben.**

You're on a tour with your dad. Listen.
Put the pictures in the right order[1]. Write 1–5.

A ☐

B ☐
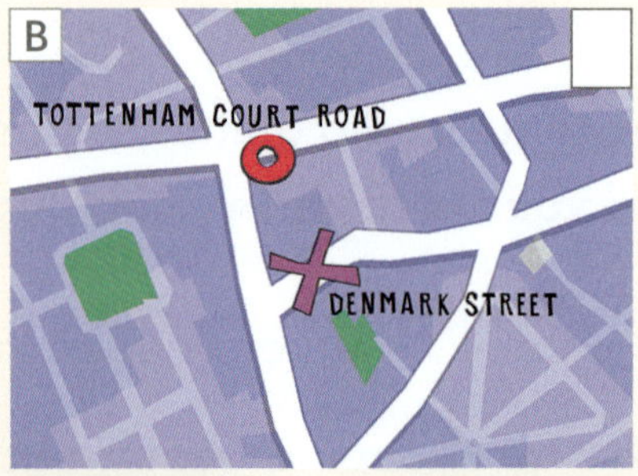


C 1

D ☐

E ☐

## 2 Words **Let's go to the South Bank**

**Ich kann über Verkehrsmittel in London reden.**

a) Complete[2] the conversation with words from the box.

hire • ticket • traffic • tube

**Lily** ______ Do you want to go to the South Bank?

**Ali** ______ Sure! Let's take the ____________ (1) to Waterloo Station.

**Lily** ______ But then I'll have to buy a ____________ (2) for the tube. Can we walk there?

**Ali** ______ Walk? That takes so long! Why don't we cycle?

**Pearl** ______ We can't ____________ (3) bikes because we're only 13. It only takes 30 minutes to walk.

**Lily** ______ Also, the ____________ (4) on the roads is horrible!

**Ali** ______ OK, let's walk!

[1] **order** *Reihenfolge* [2] **complete** *ergänzen*

Check

b) Speaking You and your friend want to travel from Camden Town to St James's Park. Partner A: You want to take the tube. Partner B: You want to walk. Act out the dialogue[1]. Partner A starts. Then swap roles[2].

| Camden Town to St James's Park | |
|---|---|
| take the tube | walk |
| 22 minutes | 55 minutes |

*It's a nice day. Do you want to go to ...?*

*Sure, let's ... It takes ...*

*I don't really want to ... Why don't we ...? It takes ...*

*That's a good idea.*

*Great, let's go!*

## 3 Language Ideas for a day in London

Ich kann eine Tour planen (conditional sentences type 1).

a) Darja and Theo are planning what to do in London. Match[3] Darja's sentences[4].

1 If we want to go shopping,
2 Maybe we'll see the King
3 If we aren't too scared,
4 And if we visit the Dungeon,

A we'll go to Camden Market.
B maybe we'll see a ghost!
C if we go to Buckingham Palace.
D we'll visit the London Dungeon.

b) Now complete Theo's sentences. Use the simple present.

1 If you *go* _____ (go) to the Dungeon, I'll stay outside!
2 If we ________ (stop) at Hyde Park, we'll see the Princess Diana memorial.
3 If it ________ (not be) sunny, we'll find a nice cafe.
4 If we ________ (travel) by tube, we won't get tired.

[1] **dialogue** *Dialog* [2] **role** *Rollen* [3] **match** *zuordnen* [4] **sentence** *Satz*

Check

# United

## A magazine for young people across the UK

### Multicultural London *by Pearl Cole*

*I love that people in my city come from all over the world!*
*Look at this map of London: It shows the main languages[1] that people speak (after English).*

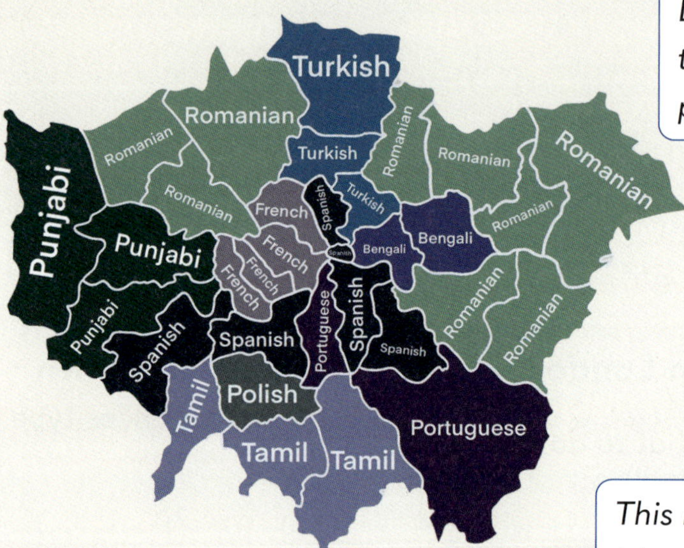


Datenquelle: Office for National Statistics in London: https://www.ons.gov.uk/datasets/TS024/editions/2021/versions/1#version-history

*This is my favourite poem[2].*
*It's called "All in this together," by Zaina.*
*She was twelve when she wrote it.*

***All in this together** by Zaina (12)*

*Once[3] I walked down the lane[4]*
*and I heard somebody say*
*I am Chinese, Japanese, German,*
*Spanish, French*
*but it doesn't matter who you are, or*
*what language you speak …*
*(…)*
*Everybody can speak this language*
*Old or young or smart or not.*
*If we smile and laugh and*
*love each other*
*It's clear what we're going to say.*

*We are all in this together*
*doesn't matter[5] who you are*
*doesn't matter what you speak or say*
*if you laugh or cry[6] or love or play …*
*(…)*

**In how many languages can you say 'Hello'?**

[1] **language** *Sprache* [2] **poem** *Gedicht* [3] **once** *einmal* [4] **lane** *Straße*
[5] **(it) doesn't matter** *(es) ist egal* [6] **cry** *weinen*

## Let me tell you more about …

### London's multicultural communities

*Over the years, Britain has needed workers for many different jobs. That's one reason why there are so many multicultural communities in London. My great-grandparents came from Jamaica in the 1950s to work here.*

*Brick Lane is a street in London famous for its big Bangladeshi community. My friend Lahari's grandparents lived near Brick Lane. They worked very hard so that their children[1] could have a better life. Lahari and I go to Brick Lane to enjoy the best curry in Britain.*

*The Chinese community has been in London for a very long time – since[2] the1800s! Today's Chinatown started in the 1970s, but now Chinese Londoners live and work all over the city. There are more than 80 restaurants and I love to go there with my family.*

*My neighbour Zuzia is from Poland. She came to London with her family. Her dad is a builder, and he has started his own business. This is her mum's Polish food shop.*

[1] **children** *Kinder*  [2] **since** *seit*

# Partner page

▸ page 17

## My task

### 5 What's the best transport[1]?

**Partner B:** You're at Camden Market. You want to go to Oxford Street with your partner. Look at the table. Answer partner A's questions. Then you ask the questions. Complete[2] the table.

**Partner B:** *How long does it take to go by bus / tube?*
**Partner A:** *It takes ... minutes.*
**Partner B:** *How much does it cost?*
**Partner A:** *It costs ... pounds/ pence.*

| Camden Market to Oxford Street (3 km) | bus | tube | taxi | walk |
|---|---|---|---|---|
| Time | ______ | ______ | 6 min. | 36 min. |
| Price | free for kids | ______ | £10 | ______ |

# Extra practice

## Extra practice 1

▸ page 14

Listen again and choose A or B. Circle[3] the right answer.

1 Big Ben tells you A the time B the date.

2 The royal family lives at A Buckingham Palace B the Elizabeth Tower.

3 The Tower of London is interesting if you like A old buildings B stairs.

4 The London Eye is a tall A door B wheel.

5 Ali's favourite thing to do at Camden Market is to A eat food B shop.

[1] **transport** *Verkehrsmittel* [2] **complete** *ergänzen* [3] **circle** *umkreisen*

## Extra practice 2

▶ page 16

**Ali's friend Mo from Canada is in London.**
**Complete[1] the sentences[2]. Use the verbs in the box.**

| |
|---|
| buy • cross • drive • hire • take |

**Ali** ______ At the weekend we can __________ (1) bikes and see the real London!

**Mo** ______ Great! But I'm really tired now. Can we take a taxi?

**Ali** ______ Taxis cost a lot of money, and they're not very green. Let's __________ (2) the tube.

**Mo** ______ OK. But I need to __________ (3) a ticket.

**Ali** ______ No problem. The station is over there, we need to __________ (4) the road here. Careful – cars __________ (5) on the left here, remember?

**Mo** ______ Oh yes, thanks!

## Extra practice 3

▶ page 16

**Make a mind map with transport[3] words and phrases[4]. Use the words from page 16.**

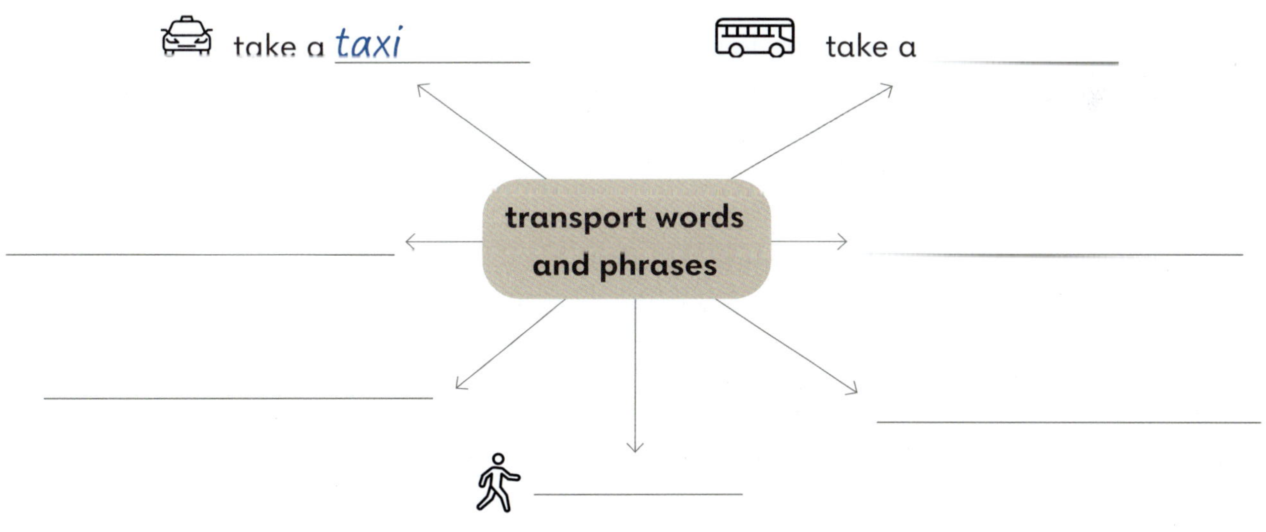


[1] **complete** *ergänzen* [2] **sentence** *Satz* [3] **transport** *Verkehrsmittel* [4] **phrase** *Redewendung*

## Extra practice 4

▶ page 17

**Read 1–6. What will you do? Match[1].**

| | |
|---|---|
| 1 Someone is calling you on the phone. | A "I won't just wear a T-shirt! I'll wear warm clothes." |
| 2 You don't understand your English teacher. | B "I'll ask her to say the question again." |
| 3 It's cold outside. | C "I'll help him." |
| 4 Your friend invites you to her birthday party. | D "I'll go to bed now." |
| 5 Your dad is cleaning the kitchen. | E "I'll buy a present for my friend." |
| 6 You're feeling very tired. | F "I'll answer and see who it is." |

## Extra practice 5

▶ page 17

**Lily has questions for Ali and Pearl. Use the verbs in the box for Ali and Pearl's answers.**

will be • ~~will we~~ • won't buy • 'll do • 'll leave • 'll think

**Lily** Where *will we* (1) go first?

**Pearl** Let's look at the food first.

**Lily** Will there be a lot of people?

**Ali** Yes, there ____________ (2) a lot of people!

**Lily** Will you buy something, Pearl?

**Pearl** No, I ____________ (3) anything today.

**Lily** How long will we be at the market?

**Ali** We____________ (4) when you want to!

**Lily** What will we do after the market?

**Pearl** We____________ (5) something fun – what about Oxford Street?

**Lily** How will we travel to Oxford Street?

**Ali** We____________ (6) about that later.

[1] **match** *zuordnen*

## Extra practice 6

▸ page 18

a) **Read and look at the photos. Then match[1] the places (1–6) to the photos (A–F). Write A–F next to the correct[2] place.**

1 Buckingham Palace C
2 London Dungeon ☐
3 Oxford Street ☐
4 Tower Bridge ☐
5 Tower of London ☐
6 Trafalgar Square ☐

A

This is a museum about the history of London. Careful – it's very scary!

B

This is a very old castle with the word "tower" in its name. Some people think there are ghosts here!

C

This is the King's biggest home. It's also where he meets important people.

D

This is one of the most famous bridges in London. You can walk, cycle or drive across its two towers.

E

This is a famous place with a very tall statue. It's a good place to meet friends.

F

This is a famous street for shopping. There are lots of shops here – and it's always very busy!

[1] **match** *zuordnen* [2] **correct** *richtig*

## Extra practice 7

▸ page 19

**Complete[1] the if-sentences[2] (conditional sentences). Use *’ll* or *won’t*.**

1 If my friend goes to London, she *’ll travel* (travel) on the underground.

2 If she travels on the underground, she ______________ (buy) a ticket.

3 If she buys a ticket, she ______________ (not have) money to buy a cool T-shirt.

4 She ______________ (not be) happy if she doesn’t buy a T-shirt.

5 So I think if she goes to London, she ______________ (walk) – because it’s free!

## Extra practice 8

▸ page 28

**Match[3] the words to the right pictures.**

| | |
|---|---|
| 1 department store | A  |
| 2 doorkeeper | B  |
| 3 sunglasses | C   |
| 4 fountain | D   |
| 5 statue | E  |

[1] **complete** *ergänzen* [2] **sentence** *Satz* [3] **match** *zuordnen*

## Hello! Where we're from

| | | |
|---|---|---|
| ▶ p. 10 | **Great Britain** | Großbritannien |
| | **island** | die Insel |
| | **Ireland** | Irland |
| | **the United Kingdom (the UK)** | das Vereinigte Königreich |
| | **Northern Ireland** | Nordirland |
| | **Scotland** | Schottland |
| | **republic** | die Republik |
| ▶ p. 12 | **bagpipes** *(pl)* | der Dudelsack |

**bagpipes**

| | | |
|---|---|---|
| | **modern** | modern |
| ▶ p. 13 | **boat** | das Boot; das Schiff |

a **boat**

## Unit 1
## London: City life

| | | |
|---|---|---|
| ▶ p. 14 | **sight** | die Sehenswürdigkeit |
| | **parliament** | das Parlament |
| | **famous** | berühmt |
| ▶ p. 15 | **royal** | königlich |
| | **palace** | der Palast, das Schloss |
| | **tower** | der Turm |

a **tower**

| | | |
|---|---|---|
| | **wheel** | das Rad |
| | **market** | der Markt |

## Topic 1

| | | |
|---|---|---|
| ▶ p. 16 | **public transport** | die öffentlichen Verkehrsmittel |
| | **tube** | die Londoner U-Bahn |
| | **underground** | die U-Bahn |
| | **way** | die Art und Weise |
| | (to) **hire** | mieten, leihen |

| | | | |
|---|---|---|---|
| | **traffic** | der (Straßen-)Verkehr | |
| | **careful** | vorsichtig | |
| | **if** | wenn, falls | |
| | (to) **drive, drove** | *(mit dem Auto)* fahren | |
| | **before you cross the road** | bevor du die Straße überquerst | |
| | (to) **cross** | kreuzen, überqueren | |
| | **road** | die Straße *(in oder zwischen Orten)* | |
| ▸ p. 17 | (to) **cost, cost** | kosten | |
| | **price** | der (Kauf-)Preis | |

## Topic 2

| | | | |
|---|---|---|---|
| ▸ p. 18 | **ghost** | der Geist, das Gespenst |  a **ghost** |
| | **dungeon** | der Kerker, das Verlies *(in einer Burg)* | |
| | **beautiful** | schön, wunderschön | |
| | **prime minister** | der Premierminister, die Premi-erministerin | |
| ▸ p. 19 | **king** | der König | |
| | **flag** | die Fahne, die Flagge | |

## Topic 3

| | | | |
|---|---|---|---|
| ▸ p. 22 | **chickpea** | die Kichererbse |  **chickpeas** |
| | **cucumber** | die Gurke *(Salatgurke)* |  a **cucumber** |
| | **spicy** | würzig | |
| | **bottomless** | mit kostenlosem Nachschank *(bei Getränken z.B. in Cafés)* | |
| | **coffee** | der Kaffee | |
| | **Could I have ...?** | Könnte ich ... bekommen? | |
| ▸ p. 23 | **waiter, waitress** | der Kellner, die Kellnerin |  a **waitress** |

| | | |
|---|---|---|
| | **everything** | alles |
| | **careless** | unvorsichtig, leichtsinnig |
| | (to) **order** | bestellen |
| | **Would you like anything else?** | Möchten Sie sonst noch etwas? |
| ▸ p. 24 | **crowd** | die (Menschen-)Menge |
| | **noise** | das Geräusch; der Lärm |
| | **smell** | der Geruch; der Gestank |
| ▸ p. 25 | **bike lane** | der Radweg |
| | **life,** *pl* **lives** | das Leben |
| | **noisy** | laut, voller Lärm; lärmend |

## Story

| | | |
|---|---|---|
| ▸ p. 26 | (to) **follow** | (be)folgen; verfolgen |
| | **department store** | das Kaufhaus |
| | (to) **be lost** | sich verlaufen/verirrt haben |
| | **well** | gut *(Adv.)* |
| ▸ p. 27 | **doorkeeper** | der Pförtner, die Pförtnerin |
| | **Excuse me, ...** | Entschuldigung, ... / Entschuldigen Sie, ... |
| | **directions** *(pl)* | die Wegbeschreibung(en) |
| | **woman,** *pl* **women** | die Frau |
| | **suddenly** | plötzlich, auf einmal |
| | **sunglasses** *(pl)* | die Sonnenbrille |
| | **princess** | die Prinzessin |

a **princess**

| | | |
|---|---|---|
| | **memorial** | das Denkmal |
| | **fountain** | der Brunnen |
| | **gate** | das Tor |
| | **water** | das Wasser |
| | **statue** | die Statue |

a **statue**

| | | |
|---|---|---|
| ▸ p. 28 | **I could** | ich konnte |
| | **quickly** | schnell *(Adv.)* |

# Unit 2
# Manchester: Who we are

**Hey!** *The online magazine of Trafford School in Manchester*

Welcome, Rosie and Omar, to our team! What's important to you?

Rosie

*Hi everyone! I'm Rosie. I'm 13, and I'm in year 9. Our planet is important to me.*

*I use a wheelchair and some people only see my disability. That's annoying! But my family and friends are amazing. They see me: Rosie!*

our planet

my friends

*My favourite thing is my phone. My friends and I text each other every day.*

## 1 Reading **What's important to Rosie and Omar**

a) Before you read **Look at the pictures on pages 44–45. What can you see?**

b) **Read about Rosie and Omar. Then complete[1] the sentences[2] with the blue words.**

Rosie is 13 and she's in year 9. ________________ is important to her.

Her family and her ____________ are amazing.

Omar is 13 and he's in year 9 too. His __________ is important to him.

______________ is his favourite city.

---

[1] **complete** *ergänzen* [2] **sentence** *Satz*

## Nach dieser Unit kann ich ...

- ○ erklären, was mir wichtig ist
- ○ über Mode reden
- ○ Ratschläge geben
- ○ über Selbstbewusstsein sprechen
- ○ einen Konflikt besprechen
- ○ meine Meinung ausdrücken

## Unit task

- ○ an einer Diskussion teilnehmen

## 2 Speaking **What's important to you**

**a)** What is important to you? Circle[1].

| |
|---|
| bike • computer • family • pet • phone • skateboard |

| |
|---|
| cousins • friends • hobbies • parents • teachers |

**b)** Tell a partner what is important to you.

*My ... is important to me.*

*My ... are important to me.*

▶ Extra practice 1, p. 64

[1] circle *umkreisen*

Digital quiz Ich kann erklären, was mir wichtig ist.

# Manchester fashion

## 1 Listening **Omar's interviews**

a) Before you listen **What clothes and colours do you see? Write the colours. Tell a partner.**

b) **Listen. Look at the photos in a) and write A–D next to the correct[1] name.**

1 Eliza ☐   2 Neil ☐   3 Richard ☐   4 Maya ☐

c) **Listen again. Who says it? Write E (Eliza), M (Maya), N (Neil) or R (Richard).**

1 I sometimes borrow clothes from my sister. ☐

2 A cool brand at a good price is the best. ☐

3 It's cold today! But my sweater is warm. ☐

4 I love these trousers. ☐

▶ Wordbank 3, p. 142

## 2 Compare[2] the outfits

Erklär-film

**Complete[3] the sentences[4].**

| nicer • most comfortable |
|---|

1 Black shoes are ____________ (nice) than trainers.

2 Neil's outfit is the ____________ (comfortable).

▶ Extra practice 2, p. 65

**Remember**

cool
cooler than
the coolest

boring
more boring than
the most boring

[1] **correct** *korrekt* [2] **compare** *vergleichen* [3] **complete** *ergänzen* [4] **sentence** *Satz*

## 3 Words **Describing clothes**

Make a mind map with words that describe clothes.
You can use words from page 46.

## My task

### 4 My fashion

You choose Do A or B. Look at 3 for ideas.

**A** Answer these questions: What are your favourite clothes? Where do you like to buy your clothes? Complete the sentences. Tell a partner.

*My favourite clothes are my* ____________________ *because they are* ____________________. *I* ____________________ *(always / often / never) buy my clothes* ____________________.

▸ Wordbank 3, p. 142

**B** You need a new outfit for a party, but you don't have a lot of money to spend. What are you going to do? Tell a partner. Start with: *I'm going to …*

borrow something from … •
go to a clothes swap • go to a charity shop •
make … cooler with a …

▸ Digital help

Digital quiz Ich kann über Mode reden.

# Family, friendship[1] and love

## 1 Reading I need some advice!

a) Before you read **What do you think? Read question 1 and 2. Tick[2] (✓), then check with your partner.**

1 What's the worst problem for teenagers?

A bullies ☐ B homework ☐ C family ☐

2 What's is the best place to get advice?

A online ☐ B parents ☐ C friends ☐

b) ***Hey! Magazine*** **gives students advice. Read the messages 1–3. What is the correct[3] heading[4]? Write A–C in the boxes.**

A Problems with parents   B Problems with school   C More than friends?

www. hey-trafford-school.example.net/advice

1 ☐
**Dear *Hey! Magazine***
School is hard for me right now. I'm often very tired, and I don't understand my lessons. I'm going to go to the homework club next week. Do you have any other ideas?
Worried student 🙄

2 ☐
**Dear *Hey! Magazine***
My parents have so many rules and we fight a lot. They always ask me, 'Is your phone going to be on? Are you going to be home on time?' I get so angry!
Angry student 😤

3 ☐
**Dear *Hey! Magazine***
I like this girl in my class. It's usually hard for me to talk to people. But with her, it's easy. I'm going to go to the cinema with her and some friends this Friday. Should I tell her how I feel? What if she doesn't like me back?
Student with a crush ❤

[1] **friendship** *Freundschaft* [2] **tick** *abhaken* [3] **correct** *korrekt* [4] **heading** *Überschrift*

## 2 Mediation Lots of problems

**What are the problems in messages 1–3 on page 48? Write in German.**

In Nachricht 1 sucht eine Person Hilfe, weil sie ______________________.

In Nachricht 2 hat eine Person ein Problem mit ______________________.

In Nachricht 3 braucht eine Person Rat, weil ______________________.

## 3 What about you?

**What's the best answer for questions 1–3? Tick (✓) A or B. Work with a partner.**

1 What can you do to stop fighting with your parents?
A Don't talk at all. ☐ B Tell them how you feel. ☐

2 If a friend has a problem, what do you do?
A Don't talk with your friend. ☐ B Talk with your friend alone. ☐

3 How does a good friend make you feel?
A Happy and confident. ☐ B Unhappy and uncool. ☐

## 4 Looking at language The going to-future

Erklär-film

**Read sentences[1] 1 and 2. Then circle[2] the right answer A, B or C in the box.**

1 I'm going to go to the homework club.
2 I'm going to go to the cinema with her.

Mit dem *going-to*-Futur sprechen wir über

A die Vergangenheit. B die Gegenwart. C Pläne für die Zukunft.

Wir bilden das *going-to*-Futur mit *am*, *is* oder *are* + *going to* + Verb.

**Remember**

Die Kurzformen von *am*, *is*, *are* sind:
*am* = *'m*
*is* = *'s*
*are* = *'re*

▸ Extra practice 3–4, p. 66

[1] **sentence** *Satz* [2] **circle** *umkreisen*

## 5 Talking about the problems

**Complete[1] the sentences with *'m / is / 're*.**

**Omar** What do you think about the first message? The person *is* (1) going to go to the homework club. That's good!

**Rosie** I agree. But I don't have any other ideas.

**Omar** Giving advice is hard.

**Rosie** Ms Hall _____ (2) going to write the answers with us. She'll know what to say.

**Omar** That's true. We_____ (3) going to talk to her tomorrow.

**Rosie** And later I_____ (4) going to spend some time online. Maybe I can find more ideas.

## 6 Listening Crushes

a) Before you listen **Can you remember: What's a 'crush'? Circle the right answer.**

A A bully. B A person that you like. C A person that is leaving school.

b) **Listen and write. True (T) or false[2] (F)?**

1 Rosie has a crush on somebody. ☐

2 Rosie thinks that Lisa has to talk with Alex's crush. ☐

3 Alex and his crush are going to the cinema. ☐

4 Maybe Alex's crush likes him too. ☐

c) **Complete the questions with *going to*. Then listen again and check.**

1 Are you *going to* tell her how you feel?

2 Is Lisa _____________ tell your crush the truth?

3 Are you _____________ watch a film with her?

[1] **complete** *ergänzen* [2] **false** *falsch*

## 7 Reading **Giving advice**

a) **This chat program gives advice. Read the chat. What is SadGirl's problem?**

| | |
|---|---|
| SadGirl | I don't like my body. |
| *Hey!* | I'm sorry that you feel bad. |
| SadGirl | I run every day and I only eat healthy food. But it's not working. |
| *Hey!* | Sport is great! But you shouldn't run every day. You should rest too. You should eat healthy food, but you can eat chips and sweets sometimes too. |
| SadGirl | OK, I'm going to run three times a week. And I'm going to eat food that I like too. |
| *Hey!* | Good. You should be kind to yourself! |
| SadGirl | I have an idea. When I look at myself in a mirror, I'm going to think about what I like. |
| *Hey!* | I really like that idea. |

b) **What advice does *Hey!* give? Look at the blue words in a).**

*You should rest … You shouldn't …*

We use *should* and *shouldn't* to give advice.

▸ Extra practice 5, p. 67

### My task

## 8 Make a plan

**Choose a problem (A, B or C). What can you do about this problem? Make a plan. Use the ideas in 1–8 and the going to-future.**

A My friend is sad. B School is too hard

C My parents have too many rules.

▸ Digital help

| | | | |
|---|---|---|---|
| 1 … ask if she/he wants to talk. | 2 … stay calm and listen to their opinion. | 3 … talk to a teacher about it. | 4 … say that I want to help her/him. |
| 5 … tell my parents how I feel. | 6 … ask a friend to help me. | 7 … do fun things with her/him. | 8 … ask for new rules. |

*My problem is that* ______________________.

*First, I'm going to* ______________________.

*Then* ______________________.

Digital quiz Ich kann **Pläne machen.**

# Confidence

## 1 Listening Mei's school radio podcast

a) Before you listen **What is a podcast? Circle[1] A, B or C.**

A A pantomime. B You listen to it. C A shop.

b) **Listen to Mei's podcast. Circle the correct[2] answers.**

Mei is in year 12 at Rosie and Omar's school.

1 Today Mei is talking about
A school B confidence on her podcast.

2 When she was younger, Mei
A had lots of friends B felt different.

3 So she joined a A football team B new band.

4 Mei asks everyone to A look after themselves B choose a song.

## 2 Looking at language Reflexive pronouns

a) **Listen to Mei's podcast in 1b) again and put the sentences[3] in the right order.**

A A lot of people don't like themselves at some time in their lives. ☐

B I want you all to look after yourselves! ☐

C If you don't believe in yourself, it can be a big problem. 1

D Omar listens to it when he doesn't believe in himself. ☐

b) **Complete[4] the table[5] with the blue words (reflexive pronouns) in a).**

| | | | |
|---|---|---|---|
| I | myself | it | itself |
| you | ______ | we | ourselves |
| he | ______ | you (all) | ______ |
| she | herself | they | ______ |

They are looking at themselves in the mirror.

[1] **circle** *umkreisen* [2] **correct** *korrekt* [3] **sentence** *Satz* [4] **complete** *ergänzen* [5] **table** *Tabelle*

## 3 Feel more confident

**Read the sentences and circle the correct blue words (reflexive pronouns).**

1 Mei wants people to believe in himself / themselves .

2 If you don't like ourselves / yourself , it makes you feel bad.

3 That's why Mei says, 'It's important to me that I like itself / myself .'

4 'And we have to take care of ourselves / themselves!'

▸ Extra practice 6, p. 67

## 4 Reading **A confidence role model**[1]

a) Before you read **Think of confident people. Brainstorm with the class.**

b) **Read about Marcus Rashford.**

### Marcus Rashford: Champion of confidence

Marcus Rashford is a footballer – but he isn't only a footballer! He's an amazing player for Manchester United and he helps poor kids all over the UK to get free meals. He believes that we all need to help each other – just like a football team.

Rashford is very busy! He wrote two books about confidence. In these books, he helps young people to believe in themselves.

Rashford also has problems in his life. Sometimes people are racist to him, but now he's more confident than ever. He says, 'Whenever I hear *no*, I ask myself: *why not*?'

Marcus, all your fans here in Manchester are proud of you!

c) **Write true (T) or false[2] (F).**

1 Rashford only plays football. F

2 He plays for Manchester City. ☐

3 His charity gives food to poor kids. ☐

4 He is also a writer. ☐

5 People are racist to him. ☐

6 His fans don't like him. ☐

[1] **role model** *Rollenmodel* [2] **false** *falsch*

## 5 Song *Brave*

Sara Bareilles

a) Before you listen **Watch the first minute of the music video *Brave* by Sara Bareilles with no sound[1]. What do you think: How do the dancers in the video feel?**

*I think they feel …*

| bored • brave • confident • happy • … |
|---|

▸ Wordbank 4, p. 143

b) **Now listen to the song. What is the message? Circle A, B or C.**

A I don't feel very confident.

B We should all be the same.

C You should believe in yourself.

## 6 Viewing **Ways to appear confident**

a) Before you watch **When do you feel confident? Circle A, B or C. You can write your own idea in D.**

A When I wear my favourite clothes.

B When I'm with my best friend.

C When I do sport.

D ____________________

b) **Watch the video. Do you think Sammy is confident? Circle.** Yes No

c) **Watch again. Complete the tips[2] with the words in the box.**

| clothes • loudly • people • straight • yourself |
|---|

1 Stand up ____________. ☐

2 Speak clearly and ____________. ☐

3 Repeat ____________. ☐

4 Don't interrupt ____________. ☐

5 Wear ____________ that make you feel good. ☐

6 Smile. ☐

d) **Draw ☺ next to the three tips[2] you think are the best.**

[1] **sound** *Ton* [2] **tip** *Tipp*

## 7 Speaking **Compliments**

Mei always gives compliments to other students in her podcast.

a) Make compliments. First, draw lines[1].

| | | |
|---|---|---|
| I think you're | | dancing • playing football • singing • ... |
| You're great at | | kind • funny • clever • nice • ... |

b) Give each other compliments. Use the sentences in a). Say 'Thank you'!

*Hi, Suki. I think you are very clever.*

*Thank you, Atalay!*

### My task

## 8 Role-play **Being confident**

a) In groups of three, write two tips for being more confident. The ideas in 6c) can help you.

1 ______________________

2 ______________________

b) Act out a short role-play[2]:

1 Student A meets student B. Student B isn't confident.

2 Student C gives student B two tips for being confident.

3 Students A and B repeat part 1. This time, student B uses the tips and is more confident.

c) Do your role-play for another group.

d) Give the other group a compliment about their role-play.

*You had good tips. / You spoke loudly. / ...*

[1] **line** *Linie* [2] **role-play** *Rollenspiel*

Digital quiz Ich kann über Selbstbewusstsein sprechen.

# A Manchester match

## 1 Before you read Sports and games

What is your favourite sport or game? Tell a partner.

*I love to ...*

A 
do karate

B 
play football

C 
dance

D 
play games

E 
skateboard

F 
play games

G 
swim

H 
play basketball

I 
run

▸ Wordbank 6, p. 145

## 2 Reading Omar's favourite team

**Read the story.**

Omar was so excited. Today was the football match between Manchester City and Manchester United. Omar, his dad and his sister had tickets for the match. He put on his blue Manchester City football shirt and his scarf.

They took the bus to the stadium and walked in with lots of Manchester City fans.

'We are City, super City, from Maine Road,' sang the fans and Omar sang with them. 'City, City, the best team in the land, in all the world.'

Omar got a text from his friend Trent:

*May the best team win! (That's United of course!)*

Trent's cousin Ollie was a Manchester United fan. They were at the match too. Omar read the message and laughed. 'In your dreams, Trent!' he thought.

At half-time the score was 0–0. Omar, his sister and his dad bought hot dogs. 'It's a hard match,' said Omar's dad.

'I know ... but City will win!' said Omar's sister.

The rest of the match was fast and exciting. The fans sang and Omar was full of love for his team. Then United scored a goal.

'Yes!' cheered the Manchester United fans. Omar felt horrible. Then he got a new text from Trent:

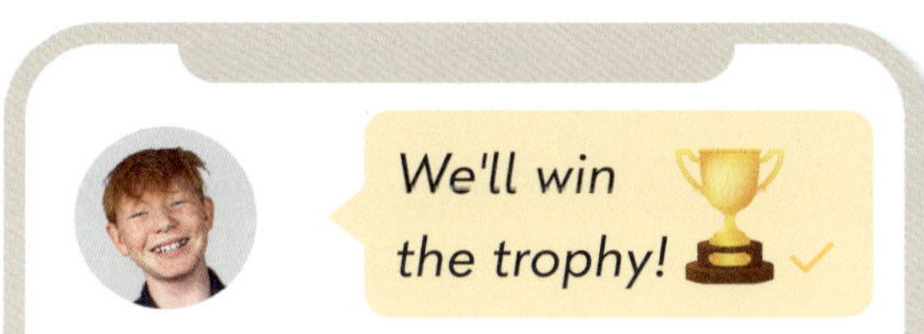


Omar felt angry with Trent. Two minutes later, Manchester City scored a goal. Omar cheered and texted Trent back:

The match was almost over. The score was 1–1. Omar was worried ... But then Manchester City scored again! Omar, his dad and his sister hugged each other. All of the City fans jumped and sang.

Later, outside the stadium, there were people everywhere. Some unhappy Manchester United fans called the Manchester City fans horrible names and took their scarves. Omar's dad said, 'Just keep walking.'

Omar saw Trent and waved to him, but Trent looked down. At first, Omar didn't understand why.

But then Ollie, who was next to Trent, saw Omar. Ollie had a mean smile on his face and called Omar racist names.

Omar felt hot. He was angry and hurt. He went to Trent and looked at him. Omar asked, 'Are you my friend or not?'

## 3 What happened

**Put the sentences[1] A–E in the right place on the timeline[2].**

| Before the match | At the start of the match | At half-time | At the end of the match | After the match |
|---|---|---|---|---|
| C | | | | |

A Trent's cousin Ollie was horrible to Omar.

B Trent sent Omar a message that United is the best team.

C Omar put on his Manchester City clothes.

D Manchester City scored again.

E there were no goals.

▸ Extra practice 7, p. 68

## 4 Are you my friend?

**At the end Omar asks Trent, 'Are you my friend or not?' What does Omar mean? Circle[3] A or B.**

A I don't want to be your friend because your cousin is a bully.

B You aren't a good friend because you aren't helping me.

## 5 Freeze!

**Look at the blue sentences in the story. Choose one with your group and show it as a freeze-frame[4]. The other groups find the sentences in the story and read them out loud.**

## 6 The ending[5]

a) **What do you think happened next? Talk to a partner.**

| | |
|---|---|
| Maybe | Trent told Ollie to stop. |
| | Ollie walked away. |
| I think | Trent said sorry to Omar. |

b) **Listen to what happened. Do you like your ending or the one you just heard?**

[1] **sentence** *Satz* [2] **timeline** *Zeitleiste* [3] **circle** *umkreisen* [4] **as a freeze-frame** *als Standbild*
[5] **ending** *Ende*

Digital quiz Ich kann einen Konflikt besprechen.

# Coach

## 1 Football fans

Before you watch **Are you a football fan?**

| exciting • boring • cool • mean • ... |
|---|

I think football is ________________.

In my opinion, football fans are ________________.

## 2 Viewing What happens

a) **Watch the film.**

b) **What's the right order? Write 1–6. Then check.**

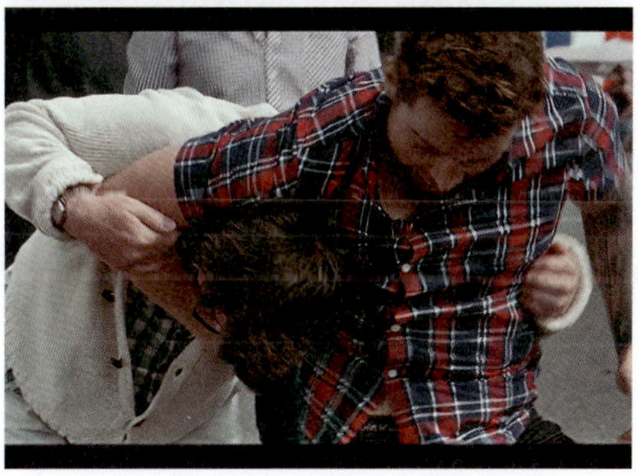

A David and his dad are going to a football match. Then there's a problem with the car. [1]

B David sees the fight and helps his dad. The police stop the fight. [ ]

C David gets back on the coach alone. His dad and one of the fans start to fight. [ ]

D The coach stops and everyone gets out. David's dad wants to leave. [ ]

E They get on a coach with lots of loud football fans. [ ]

F The police drive all of them back to Calais. [ ]

## 3 What do you think?

**How does David feel? Draw lines[1].**

| | |
|---|---|
| 1 When there's a problem with the car. | A excited |
| 2 When he gets into the bus and the fans are singing. | B tired |
| 3 At the end of the film when they are back on the coach. | C angry |

[1] **line** *Linie*

# Giving opinions

## 1 Give your opinion

Look at 1. How do we say what we think? Underline[1] the words in 2 and 3.

▸ Extra practice 8, p. 68

1 *I think football is the best sport …*

2 *In my opinion, ketchup on pasta is the best …*

3 *If you ask me, snakes are scary …*

## 2 Give reasons[2]

Match A–C to the opinions in 1. Write 1–3.

A … because they move very fast. ☐

B … because I like tomatoes. ☐

C … because it's exciting when my team scores goals. ☐

## 3 Agree or disagree[3]

Do we say sentences 1–4 to agree or disagree? Draw ☺ for agree and ☹ for disagree.

1 Maybe you're right. ☐

2 I don't agree with you at all. ☐

3 Sorry, I think you're wrong. ☐

4 I completely agree. ☐

## 4 Walk around **Quick opinions**

Your teacher says two things, for example 'cats and dogs'. Say what you think. Change[4] the words in blue. Your partner agrees or disagrees.

*In my opinion, dogs are better than cats.*

*I completely agree!*

*I don't agree with you at all.*

[1] **underline** *unterstreichen* [2] **reason** *Grund* [3] **disagree** *anderer Meinung sein* [4] **change** *verändern*

Digital quiz — Ich kann meine Meinung sagen und sie begründen.

# Have a discussion[1]

## Step[2] 1

You're going to have a discussion about school uniforms. Read sentences[3] 1–4. Underline[4] the sentences that are for uniforms in green and against school uniforms in blue. Check with a partner.

1 It's easier to get dressed in the mornings.
2 I use clothes to show other people who I am.
3 You feel like you're part of the school.
4 It's hard to buy school uniforms second-hand.

*Right. And number … is against them.*

*I think number … is for school uniforms.*

▸ Digital help

## Step 2

Have a discussion with your partner. Partner A is for school uniforms. Use the green sentences in Step 1. Partner B is against school uniforms. Use the blue sentences in Step 1.

**Partner A** *I believe that school uniforms are good because …*
**Partner B** *I don't agree with you at all. I think that …*
**Partner A** *Sorry, I think you're wrong. In my opinion, …*
**Partner B** *If you ask me, school uniforms are bad because …*

▸ Digital help

## Step 3

Opinion line What's your opinion? Are school uniforms a great or a horrible idea for your school? Say what you think, listen to what the others think, then stand in a line[5].

a great idea | a good idea | I'm not sure | a boring idea | a horrible idea

[1] **have a discussion** *eine Diskussion führen* [2] **step** *Schritt* [3] **sentence** *Satz*
[4] **underline** *unterstreichen* [5] **stand in a line** *in einer Reihe stehen*

Digital quiz

Ich kann an einer Diskussion teilnehmen.

## 1 Listening **Mei's podcast**

Ich kann erklären, was mir wichtig ist.

**Listen. What's the correct[1] picture (A–F) for Ethan, Hafsa, Ryan and Laura? There are two extra pictures.**

Ethan D Hafsa ☐ Ryan ☐ Laura ☐

A my team

B my phone

C travel

D my home

E my friends

F my grandma and grandpa

## 2 Words **What are they wearing?**

Ich kann über Mode reden.

**Match[2] the clothes to the people.**

| A | B | C | D | E | F |
|---|---|---|---|---|---|
| • black hoodie<br>• blue jeans | • yellow shirt<br>• brown shorts | • green dress<br>• green shoes | • orange jacket<br>• yellow trousers | • blue sweater<br>• grey trousers | • black jacket<br>• green trousers |

[1] **correct** *richtig* [2] **match** *zuordnen*

Check

## 3 Language Aya's problem

Ich kann Pläne machen.

Complete[1] Zoe and Aya's messages.
Use the going-to future.

**Zoe** ____ Hey Aya, are you OK? I heard that Josh was mean to you again.

**Aya** ____ Hey Zoe. He was horrible. 😤 I don't know what I ______________ (1) do.

**Zoe** ____ He ______________ (2) keep doing this, you know. I think you have to talk to someone. What about Ms Thomas? She's nice.

**Aya** ____ You're right, she is. But I don't know what to say ...

**Zoe** ____ You ______________ (3) say, 'Ms Thomas, I have a problem.' And then you ______________ (4) tell her what he did. We ______________ (5) stop this!

**Aya** ____ OK. Thanks, Zoe! I feel better now. You're a great friend! 😊

## 4 Study skills An online profile

Ich kann meine Meinung ausdrücken.

Read the questions and Jack's opinions (1–4). Do you agree with him? Match your opinions.

| | |
|---|---|
| 1 Cats or dogs?<br>**Jack** ___ *I think that dogs are the best because you can play games with them!* | Maybe he's right. |
| 2 Football or basketball?<br>**Jack** ___ *If you ask me, football is better because it's more fun.* | Sorry, I think he's wrong. |
| 3 Sunny weather or rainy weather?<br>**Jack** ___ *I think sunny weather is better because you can go to the beach.* | I completely agree. |
| 4 Cars or bikes?<br>**Jack** ___ *In my opinion, cars are cooler because they are faster.* | I don't agree with him at all. |

[1] **complete** *ergänzen*

Check

# Extra practice

## Extra practice 1

▸ page 45

a) **Omar loves Manchester! He writes about four places. Match[1] sentences[2] 1–4 to the photos A–D.**

1 The National Football Museum is cool. It's in a big building with lots of windows.
2 I love the Trafford Centre. It's good for shopping and you can go bowling too.
3 Blackpool is a great day trip from Manchester. I love the beach and the pier there.
4 Peak District National Park is great. We went on a really cool tour – it was dark and scary!

A

B

C

D

b) **Which[3] of these places would you like to go to? Write. Then tell a partner.**

*I want to go to* ______________________________

[1] **match** *zuordnen* [2] **sentence** *Satz* [3] **which** *welche(r, s)*

## Extra practice 2

▶ page 46

**a) Compare[1] the teens in the picture.**

1 Adam's trousers are *longer* ________ (long) than Nia's trousers.

2 Nia has the ________ (short) trousers of the three teens.

3 Leo's hair is ________ (short) than Nia's hair.

4 Adam has the ________ (long) hair.

5 Nia's clothes are ________ (interesting) than Leo's clothes.

6 Adam has the ________ (interesting) clothes of the three teens.

**b) Now say what you think. Write two sentences[2].**

*Nia's trousers are cooler than Adam's trousers.*
*But Leo's trousers are the coolest.*

boring • comfortable • cool • interesting • nice • ...

Leo's clothes are ________________________________.

But Adam's jacket is the ________________________________.

[1] **compare** *vergleichen* [2] **sentence** *Satz*

## Extra practice 3

▸ page 49

**Plan your perfect weekend. Use the going to-future. Write three or four sentences[1].**

| | | |
|---|---|---|
| This weekend<br>On Saturday<br>On Sunday<br>In the morning<br>In the afternoon<br>In the evening | I'm going to<br>I'm not going to | be busy.<br>tidy my room.<br>go shopping / on a trip.<br>do homework.<br>practise football.<br>play video games.<br>... |

_______________________________________________

_______________________________________________

_______________________________________________

_______________________________________________

_______________________________________________

## Extra practice 4

▸ page 49

**Rosie is going to have a busy day! Complete[2] the sentences with the going to-future.**

In the morning Rosie *is going to take* (1 take) the bus to school because her dad can't take her by car. He ______________ (2 travel) to London for a work trip. Rosie ______________ (3 leave) at seven o'clock because she ______________ (4 do) her maths homework before class. Then she ______________ (5 go) to her first class, but she ______________ (6 not be) late. At lunch Rosie ______________ (7 meet) Omar to talk about the messages for the school magazine.

[1] **sentence** *Satz* [2] **complete** *ergänzen*

## Extra practice 5

▶ page 51

**Take turns[1] to read out a problem (1–6) or give advice with *should* or *shouldn't*. Use these ideas or your own ideas.**

1 Help! My cat can talk.
2 Help! My mum can do magic.
3 Help! There's a lion in my garden.
4 Help! I have four legs.
5 Help! My piggy bank can eat.
6 Help! My neighbours are vampires.

| | |
|---|---|
| You should<br>You shouldn't | go on TV.<br>call a vet.<br>try to run really fast.<br>go to a hospital.<br>ask your friend ... for help.<br>take pictures and sell them to a magazine. |

## Extra practice 6

▶ page 53

**Complete[2] the advice. Use the words in the box. The blue words can help you.**

| |
|---|
| himself • myself • ourselves • yourself • ~~yourselves~~ |

It's important that you all look after *yourselves* (1). We can't be really happy if we don't love ____________ (2). Of course, friends are important too, and good friends look after each other, but you should also be kind to ____________ (3). My brother says something nice to ____________ (4) in the mirror every morning. And I take care of ____________ (5) by getting lots of sleep and eating healthy food.

[1] **take turns** *wechselt euch ab* [2] **complete** *ergänzen*

## Extra practice 7

▶ page 58

**Write the words under the pictures.**

| |
|---|
| ~~fans~~ • football scarf • football shirt • score a goal • stadium • team |

A

fans

B

C

D

E

F

## Extra practice 8

▶ page 60

**How do we say what we think? Underline[1] the words. Then tick[2] (✓) the boxes that you agree with.**

1 If you ask me, Döner is better than pizza. ☐
2 I think that friends are more important than family. ☐
3 If you ask me, apple juice is nicer than cola. ☐
4 In my opinion, beaches are more fun than mountains. ☐
5 I think that books are more interesting than toys. ☐
6 In my opinion, rap is cooler than classical music. ☐

[1] **underline** *unterstreichen* [2] **tick** *abhaken*

## Unit 2
## Manchester: Who we are

| | | |
|---|---|---|
| ▸ p. 44 | **magazine** | Zeitschrift |
| | **disability** | die Behinderung |
| | **annoying** | ärgerlich |
| ▸ p. 45 | (to) **support** | unterstützen |

## Topic 1

| | | |
|---|---|---|
| ▸ p. 46 | **ripped** | zerrissen, (ein)gerissen |
| | **skirt** | der Rock |
| | **sock** | die Socke |
| | **jacket** | die Jacke, das Jackett |
| | **comfortable** | bequem, gemütlich |
| | (to) **borrow** | (aus)leihen, sich borgen |
| | **brand** | die (Produkt-)Marke |
| ▸ p. 47 | (to) **describe** | beschreiben |

## Topic 2

| | | |
|---|---|---|
| ▸ p. 48 | **advice** *(no pl)* | der Rat, der Ratschlag, die Ratschläge |
| | **bully** | der Mobber, die Mobberin; der Tyrann, die Tyrannin |
| | **Dear …** | Liebe/r … |
| | **usually** | normalerweise, meistens |
| | **Should I …?** | Sollte ich …? |
| | **with a crush** | verliebt |
| ▸ p. 49 | **not at all** | überhaupt nicht |

| | | |
|---|---|---|
| ▸ p. 50 | (to) **have a crush** (on sb.) | in jn. verliebt sein |

| | | |
|---|---|---|
| | **crush** | der Schwarm *(jd., in den/die man verliebt ist)* |
| | **truth** | die Wahrheit |
| ▸ p. 51 | **body** | der Körper |
| | **healthy** | gesund |
| | **yourself** | dir/dich (selbst) |
| | **myself** | mir/mich (selbst) |

## Topic 3

| | | |
|---|---|---|
| ▸ p. 52 | **confidence** | das (Selbst-)Vertrauen, die Zuversicht |
| | **young** | jung |
| | (to) **join** sb./sth. | sich jm. anschließen; bei etwas mitmachen |
| | (to) **look after** sb. | sich um jn. kümmern, auf jn. aufpassen |
| | (to) **believe** (in sth.) | (an etwas) glauben |
| | **himself** | sich (selbst) |

**! Reflexive pronouns**

| | | |
|---|---|---|
| **I** | ▸ myself | mir, mich |
| **you** | ▸ yourself | dir, dich |
| **he** | ▸ himself | sich |
| **she** | ▸ herself | sich |
| **it** | ▸ itself | sich |
| **we** | ▸ ourselves | uns |
| **you** | ▸ yourselves | euch |
| **they** | ▸ themselves | sich |

| | | |
|---|---|---|
| ▸ p. 53 | (to) **take care** (of sb./sth.) | sich (um etwas/jn.) kümmern |
| | **footballer** | der/die Fußballspieler/in |
| | **player** | der Spieler, die Spielerin |
| | **poor** | arm |
| | **racist** | rassistisch |
| | **whenever** | wann (auch) immer |
| ▸ p. 54 | (to) **speak clearly** | deutlich sprechen |
| | (to) **repeat** | wiederholen |
| | (to) **interrupt** | unterbrechen |
| ▸ p. 55 | **compliment** | das Kompliment |
| | **nervous** | nervös, aufgeregt |

## Story

| | | |
|---|---|---|
| ▸ p. 56 | **excited** | aufgeregt, gespannt |
| | **scarf**, *pl* **scarves** | der Schal |

two **scarves**

| | | |
|---|---|---|
| | (to) **win, won** | gewinnen, siegen |
| ▸ p. 57 | **score** | der Spielstand |
| | (to) **score a goal** | ein Tor erzielen |

She is scoring a goal.

| | | |
|---|---|---|
| | (to) **cheer** | jubeln, *(Sportler/innen)* anfeuern |
| | **almost** | fast, beinahe |
| | (to) **hug** (sb.) | (jn.) umarmen; einander umarmen |

He is hugging his friend.

| | | |
|---|---|---|
| | (to) **call sb. names** | jn. beschimpfen |
| | (to) **keep walking** | weiter gehen |
| | (to) **wave** (to sb.) | (jm. zu)winken |

The girls are waving.

## Study skills

| | | |
|---|---|---|
| ▸ p. 60 | **completely** | völlig, absolut |

## Unit task

| | | |
|---|---|---|
| ▸ p. 61 | (to) **get dressed** | sich anziehen |
| | **against** | gegen |

**Irregular verb**

| **Infinitive** | **Simple past** | |
|---|---|---|
| (to) **feel** | **felt** | fühlen |

# Unit 3
# Scotland: Adventure

A

Inverness: The capital of the Highlands

B

Kayaking on a lake

C

Visiting Eilean Donan Castle

## 1 Listening **A school trip in Scotland**

a) Before you listen **Look at the pictures above. What can you see?**

*I can see ...*

b) **Listen to Grace and Rhona. Put the photos in the right order 1–6.**

c) **Listen again. Circle[1] the right word.**

1 Our school trip sounds[2] interesting / amazing .

2 The shops in Edinburgh are for students / tourists .

3 Eilean Donan Castle has a ghost / monster.

4 Rhona thinks that kayaking looks easy / fun.

---

[1] **circle** *umkreisen* [2] **sound** *klingen*

## Nach dieser Unit kann ich ...

- ○ über Schottland reden
- ○ Geschichten und Sagen verstehen
- ○ über Aktivitäten und Abenteuer reden
- ○ über die Natur sprechen
- ○ Entscheidungen in einer Geschichte besprechen
- ○ Ideen für eine Geschichte ordnen

## Unit task

- ○ eine kurze Abenteuergeschichte schreiben

D 1
Shopping in Edinburgh

E
Hiking on Ben Nevis (the highest mountain in the UK!)

F
Visiting Loch Ness

## 2 Speaking **Pictures of Scotland**

**Talk with a partner. Which[1] activity looks interesting to you? Why?**

| | | | |
|---|---|---|---|
| I think | visiting Inverness • kayaking on a lake • visiting Eilean Donan Castle • hiking on Ben Nevis • shopping in Edinburgh • visiting Loch Ness | looks | interesting • boring • amazing • horrible • ... |
| I like | lakes • old buildings • the sea • shopping • doing sports • being outside • ... | | |

[1] which *welche(r,s)*

Digital quiz Ich kann über Schottland reden.

# Scary Scotland

## 1 Reading The legend of the Loch Ness monster

a) Before you read Look at the picture.
What is Loch Ness? What is Nessie?
Write the words in the boxes on the picture.

b) Partner B: Look at page 94.
Partner A: Read Rhona's text on Nessie. Circle[1] A or B.

A The legend of Nessie is very popular[2]. B The loch is too small for a monster.

**Nessie: The legend** *Rhona*

Today we learned about Loch Ness and its monster, Nessie. Loch Ness is a very big lake in Scotland and it is very famous.

In 1934, a tourist took a photo of something in Loch Ness. People saw the photo and thought that it was a monster.

Some people think that Nessie is real. They think that the lake is very big, so there has to be something in it.

I think that Nessie is real because it's fun and exciting to believe in monsters.

c) Answer partner B's questions.

d) Now ask partner B these questions:

1 What is in the lake?
2 Does Grace think Nessie is real? Why or why not?

[1] **circle** *umkreisen* [2] **popular** *beliebt, populär*

## 2 Speaking My opinion about Nessie

a) Think **Do you think Nessie is real? Write one sentence[1].**

No, I don't think Nessie is real because ______________________________.

Yes, I think Nessie is real because ______________________________.

b) Pair **Tell your partner your opinion.**

c) Share **How many students in the class think Nessie is real?**

## 3 Mediation A tour of Loch Ness

a) **You want to go on this tour. Read and answer the questions in German.**

1 Wann fängt die Tour an?

______________________________

2 Wie lange dauert die Tour?

______________________________

3 Wie lange dauert die Bootsfahrt?

______________________________

**Edinburgh to Loch Ness One-Day Tour**

Enjoy beautiful Scotland with us.

Maybe you'll see Nessie too!

- *Adults: £65, children under 14: £45, babies under 1: free.*
- *We leave at 8.00 a.m. at the bus station in the centre of Edinburgh. Please don't be late! The tour takes about 12 hours.*
- *Audio guide with over 20 languages and headphones: £3.50.*
- *One-hour boat trip of Loch Ness: £18 for adults and children.*

b) **Now buy the tickets. Read the speech bubble[2] and complete[3] the dialogue[4] in English.**

Wir möchten zwei Eintrittskarten für Erwachsene und zwei für Kinder für den Tagesausflug zum Loch Ness kaufen. Dazu zwei Audioguides, aber wir wollen nicht mit auf die Bootsfahrt gehen.

**Tour guide** How can I help you?

**You** We would like to buy ______________ for adults and ______________ for children for the day trip to Loch Ness. We would also like ______________, but we don't want to go on ______________.

[1] **sentence** *Satz* [2] **speech bubble** *Sprechblase* [3] **complete** *ergänzen* [4] **dialogue** *Dialog*

## 4 Listening **Scottish ghosts**

a) Before you listen **Tell your partner what scary stories, films or series[1] you know.**

*I know a scary* ________________. *It's called* ______________________________.

b) **Listen. Grace and Rhona are at Eilean Donan Castle. True (T) or false[2] (F)?**

1 British soldiers[3] went to Spain. ☐
2 The King found out about the secret plan. ☐
3 The castle we see today is one hundred years old. ☐
4 They call the ghost Carmen. ☐

## 5 Looking at language **Adverbs of manner**

Erklär-film

a) **Read these sentences.**

| | |
|---|---|
| I'm a quiet ghost.<br>– quiet *beschreibt, wie eine Person oder eine Sache ‚ist'.* | I'm walking quietly behind you.<br>– quietly *beschreibt, wie jemand etwas tut oder wie etwas passiert.* |

b) **Read sentences 1–4. Circle the verbs and underline[4] the matching[5] adverbs. Then write the adverbs in the table on the right.**

1 I'm going to tell you a story, so listen carefully.
2 They made their plans secretly.
3 He walks slowly around the castle.
4 He carries[6] his head safely[7] under his arm.

| adjective | adverb |
|---|---|
| careful | ________ |
| secret | ________ |
| slow | ________ |
| safe | ________ |

c) **Complete[8] the rule.**

Die meisten Adverbien bilden wir, indem wir die Endung ________ an das Adjektiv anhängen.

Achtung, Ausnahmen!
good → well
It's a good story.
The guide told the ghost story well.

[1] **series** *Serie* [2] **false** *falsch* [3] **soldier** *Soldat/Soldatin* [4] **underline** *unterstreichen*
[5] **matching** *dazu passend* [6] **carry** *tragen* [7] **safe** *sicher*

## 6 The Edinburgh Castle ghost

loudly • sadly • suddenly • well

**Write the adverbs from the box in the story.**

1 A long time ago, people found tunnels[1] under Edinburgh Castle.

They wanted to make a map and asked a small boy to help because he played the bagpipes ________ (good).

2 The boy walked down the tunnels and played his bagpipes ________ (loud).

3 But then the bagpipes stopped ____________ (sudden). No one saw the boy again.

4 Today tourists often hear music. Somebody plays the bagpipes ________ (sad).

▸ Extra practice 1–2, p. 95, Extra practice 3, p. 96

## My task

## 7 My scary monster

a) **Think of a monster. Describe[2] it. Use adverbs.** ▸ Digital help

| | | |
|---|---|---|
| It | walks • talks • eats • listens • plays • runs • scares people • sings • sleeps • smiles • speaks • … | angrily. • calmly. • carefully. • happily. • loudly. • quietly. • sadly. • slowly. • … |

**My monster is the Homework Ogre..**
**He's very tall. He scares students easily.**
**He walks and talks slowly, but he eats homework quickly.**
**Students have to do their homework carefully and quietly …**
**or the Homework Ogre will eat it!**

b) **Make a poster of your monster. You can draw it or find a picture online.**

c) Gallery walk **Walk around and look at the posters. Write comments[3] on sticky notes[4].**

[1] **tunnel** *Tunnel* [2] **describe** *beschreiben* [3] **comment** *Kommentar* [4] **sticky note** *Klebezettel*

Digital quiz Ich kann **Geschichten und Sagen verstehen.**

# Outdoor activities

## 1 Listening An adventure trip

a) Before you listen **Look at the pictures. What activities can you do? Talk with a partner.**

*You can ...* *That's in picture ...*

1

jump off a cliff

2

ride a horse

3

drive a go-kart

4

sleep outside in a tent

5

hike up a mountain

6

ski down a mountain

b) **Listen. Why is Rhona worried? Circle[1].**

1 She's scared of new things. 2 She misses her pet.
3 She forgot[2] her phone at home.

c) **Listen again. Who says what? Write G (Grace) or R (Rhona).**

1 I've slept[3] outside in a tent before. ☐
2 My sister has jumped off a cliff. ☐
3 I haven't ridden a horse before. ☐
4 I've skied down a mountain. ☐

## 2 Now you

**Tell a partner which[4] activities in 1a) you want to do.**

*I want to drive a go-kart / ...* *I don't want to hike up a mountain / ...*

[1] **circle** *umkreisen* [2] **forget** *vergessen* [3] **sleep** *schlafen* [4] **which** *welche(r,s)*

## 3 Looking at language **The present perfect**

Erklär-film

**Read.**

*I've gone up lots of mountains, but **I haven't jumped** off a cliff before. Have you already done that?*

Wir verwenden das present perfect für etwas, das irgendwann oder noch nie geschehen ist. Der Zeitpunkt der Handlung ist unwichtig, aber oft hat die Handlung Folgen für die Gegenwart.

| PAST | PRESENT |
| --- | --- |
| *I've **gone** up lots of mountains,* | *No, and I don't want to try it!* |
| *but I **haven't jumped** off a cliff before.* | *It sounds really scary!* |
| ***Have** you already **done** that?* | |

Wir bilden das present perfect mit has / have und der dritten Form des Verbs (*past participle*). Regelmäßige *past participles* enden auf -ed (*looked, jumped, tried*). Manche *past participles* haben eine unregelmäßige Form (*gone, done, read*). Diese musst du lernen!

**Remember**

Die Kurzformen von *have/has*:
- *have* = *'ve*
- *has* = *'s*

Die Verneinung von *have/has*:
- *haven't*
- *hasn't*

▸ Irregular verbs, p. 138

## 4 Are you ready?

Write *have* or *haven't*.

**Grace** — Let's see. I haven't (1 not) packed my water bottle yet. I'll do that now.

**Rhona** — But I ____________ (2) remembered my warm sweater.

**Grace** — And I ____________ (3) already put[1] that in my rucksack too. Is that all?

**Rhona** — I'm sure that we ____________ (4) forgotten something!

**Grace** — I know what I ____________ (5 not) done yet[2]. The website! We ____________ (6 not) looked at it yet.

**Rhona** — That's right! Let's do that now.

▸ Extra practice 4, p. 97

[1] **I've put** *ich habe (etwas wohin) gelegt* [2] **not … yet** *noch nicht …*

## 5 Reading **The Adventure Centre's website**

a) Before you read **Look at the photos. What is Kirsten doing? Circle three right answers.**

She's at a campsite / staying in a hotel / dancing / taking photos / riding a bike / hiking / swimming.

www.example.com/adventure-team-instructors

Meet our newest instructor: *This is*

| | |
|---|---|
| *Tell us your name and your job.* | My name is Kirsten and I'm 21. I'm a new instructor. |
| *Have you ever ridden a horse?* | Yes, I have! I've ridden lots of horses. |
| *Have you ever slept in a tent?* | Yes, I have. And I've cooked many meals outside. |
| *Have you ever swum in Loch Ness?* | No, I haven't, but I've swum in really cold water. |
| *Have you ever hurt yourself?* | Yes, I've hurt my ankle. |
| *Tell us your motto.* | I think that life should be an adventure.<br>Come and have adventures with us! |

b) **Read. What has Kirsten done? Write two examples.**

She has ______________________________.

c) **Look at the website again. Kirsten answers four questions. Ask each other the questions.**

*Have you ever ridden a horse?*

*Yes, I have. / No, I haven't.*

## 6 What about you?

**The girls are talking about the website. Write the questions in the right order.**

**Grace** Some of these activities sound easier, right? Like camping, for example.

*Have you ever* ____________ (1 been camping? / you / ever / Have)

**Rhona** Yes, I have. You're right, but I didn't like it.

**Grace** Or horse riding. ____________

(2 you / ever / Have / ridden a horse?)

**Rhona** No, I haven't. But what about you, Grace? ____________

(3 ever / Have / been scared? / you)

**Grace** Yes, of course. I've been[1] scared before.

**Rhona** What about Kirsten? ____________

(4 ever / Has / been scared? / Kirsten)

**Grace** Yes, I'm sure she has been scared before! Everybody is scared sometimes.

## My task

### 7 Have you ever ...?

a) **Write three interview questions.**

*Have you ever tried skiing?*

*Yes, I have. / No, I haven't.*

▸ Digital help

| | | |
|---|---|---|
| Have you ever | tried[2] | hiking / skiing / snowboarding / surfing / ...? |
| | climbed | a mountain / a tree / ...? |
| | ridden | a horse / a pony / ...? |
| | travelled | alone / by plane / to a different country / ...? |
| | swum | in really cold water / with fish / ...? |
| | hurt | your leg / your arm / ...? |

▸ Wordbank 6, p. 145

1 ____________

2 ____________

3 ____________

b) **Ask your partner your questions. Then answer your partner's questions.**

[1] **I've been** *ich bin gewesen* [2] **I've tried** *ich habe versucht*

igital quiz Ich kann **über Aktivitäten und Abenteuer reden.**

# In nature[1]

## 1 Global goals **Protect nature**

a) **Look at the pictures and make sentences[2] with *should* or *shouldn't*.**

| | |
|---|---|
| You should | give food to farm animals. • walk on paths[3]. • leave[4] your rubbish. |
| You shouldn't | close the gates. • make a fire. • leave the flowers[5]. |

1

farm animals

2

paths

3

rubbish

4

gates

5

a fire

6

flowers

b) Words **Write the words in this table[6].**

beach • cliff • cloudy • fish • flower • goat • horse • insect • lake • mountain • mouse • rainy • river • rock • sea • seagull • snake • snowy • windy

| **Nature** | |
|---|---|
| weather | sunny, ______ |
| places in nature | the country, ______ |
| things in nature | tree, ______ |
| animals | chicken, ______ |

[1] **nature** *Natur* [2] **sentence** *Satz* [3] **path** *Pfad* [4] **leave** *zurücklassen* [5] **flower** *Blume*
[6] **table** *Tabelle*

## 2 What can we do?

a) Tick[1] (✓) the things that are good for nature.
Cross (✗) the things that are bad for nature.

1 recycle[2] ☐
2 buy lots of new things ☐
3 eat meat ☐
4 use public transport ☐
5 go by bike ☐
6 fly ☐
7 go by train ☐

b) What about you? Use the ideas in a).

*I often …* *I never …* *I try to …* *It's a good idea to …*

## My task

### 3 Nature and me

a) Think Is nature important to you? Write four sentences.
You can use the ideas in the box or your own ideas.

| | |
|---|---|
| I like to / I love to | climb a mountain • swim in a lake • go camping • … |
| I don't like to go outside because | there are a lot of insects • it's too hot • I think it's boring • … |
| Nature is important because | it gives us food / clean air[3] / clean water / … I feel great when I'm in nature / on a mountain / … |

1 ______________________

2 ______________________

3 ______________________

4 ______________________

b) Pair Talk with a partner. Say what you think. Use your sentences in a).

*Nature is / isn't important to me because …*

c) Share How many students in the class like to be in nature? How many students think that nature is important and why?

[1] **tick** *abhaken* [2] **recycle** *recyceln, wiederverwerten* [3] **air** *Luft*

Digital quiz Ich kann über die Natur sprechen.

# A mountain adventure

## 1 Reading **Preparing**[1] **for an adventure**

a) Before you read **What do you need to go hiking or mountain climbing? Look at Grace's bag and write.**

Don't forget your ______________________________________.

b) **Now read the story.**

Rhona and Grace were on the bus to Ben Nevis. Mr McAlister, one of the teachers, saw Rhona's shoes.
'Rhona, where are your walking boots? You can't wear trainers today.'
'Oh ...' Rhona's face was red.
'My walking boots are in my bag. I'll put them on later.'

Mr McAlister walked away.

Grace looked at Rhona.
'You didn't put boots in your bag this morning.'
'I know ... I don't have walking boots,' said Rhona. 'They're too expensive!'

Later, they were on the mountain. Grace was bored.
'Come on, I know a better path,' she said.
'It's harder, but it's cooler too.'
Rhona said, 'OK,' and they walked away quickly.

[1] **prepare** *sich vorbereiten (auf)*

Rhona stopped suddenly. The new path was really small and they were right next to the cliff. She could see all the way down to the valley.

'I can't do it,' she started to cry. 'It's too high. I'm really scared!' Grace took Rhona's hands and looked into her eyes. 'Breathe slowly, like me. In ... out ... in ...'

A littler later, Rhona felt better. The path got bigger again. It was still hard for Rhona because she didn't have walking boots. Then she fell.

'Ow!' said Rhona. 'Oh Grace, I'm hurt. I can't walk! I have to stop.'
'Oh no! OK, I'll call Mr McAlister,' said Grace.
Mr McAlister listened to their story.
'OK,' he said. 'A helicopter is coming now, so stay there. We'll find you.'

As they waited, they felt scared and they started to fight.
'Why did you want to go on this dangerous path?' asked Rhona.
'And, why did you wear trainers for climbing a mountain?' asked Grace.

After one hour, they heard a loud noise – it was the helicopter!

Rhona climbed into the helicopter first. Her ankle hurt a lot, but she remembered to breathe slowly. She thought, 'In ... out ... in ...,' and felt a little better.

Soon they were safely in the helicopter. Grace and Rhona didn't say anything at first. They felt tired and sad.

Suddenly, the girls looked at each other and spoke at the same time:
'Grace ...'
'Rhona ...'

They laughed.
'You go first, Grace,' said Rhona.
'What did you want to say?'

► Extra practice 5–6, p. 97

## 2 Good and bad choices[1]

Read the good 👍 and bad 👎 choices.
Was it Rhona or Grace?
Write R (Rhona) or G (Grace).

1 👎 She didn't wear the right shoes. ☐
2 👎 She wanted to leave the group. ☐
3 👍 She helped her friend to breathe. ☐
4 👍 She tried something new. ☐

## 3 Linking words

Verwende *linking words*, wenn du Texte schreibst. Deine Texte werden viel besser klingen!

a) Find and circle[2] six blue linking words on p. 85.

b) Circle the right linking word.

1 Rhona didn't buy walking boots because / and they're too expensive.
2 Grace was bored, then / so she wanted to walk on a different path.
3 Grace liked the new path, but / then it was too high for Rhona.
4 Rhona fell and / because she had to stop.

▶ Extra practice 7, p. 98

## 4 Saying sorry

At the end of the story, Grace wants to say sorry.
What was her bad choice?
Use exercise 2 for help and write.

**Grace** ___ I'm sorry that I ______________________
______________________.

**Rhona** ___ It's OK. Thank you for saying sorry.

**Grace** ___ I feel better now.

**Rhona** ___ Me too!

[1] **choice** *(Aus-)Wahl* [2] **circle** *umkreisen*

Digital quiz **Ich kann gute u. schlechte Entscheidungen in einer Geschichte besprechen.** ✓

# A road trip

## 1 Before you watch **The best way to travel**

**What's your favourite way to travel? Tell your partner.**

*My favourite way to travel is by ...*

bike • bus • car • plane • train • ...

## 2 Viewing **Sightseeing**

a) **Watch the video. What do Mon and Jorge see? Tick[1] (✓).**

1 a bridge ☐ 2 a city ☐ 3 a lake ☐
4 a valley ☐ 5 a fire ☐ 6 a castle ☐

b) **Watch the video again. Circle the right answer A or B.**

| | | |
|---|---|---|
| 1 What is Scotland famous for? | A castles | B tea |
| 2 What city do they stop in? | A Inverness | B Edinburgh |
| 3 What haven't they seen today? | A horses | B monsters |
| 4 What do they have a lot of for the next vlog? | A videos | B ideas |

## 3 Scottish activities

listen to bagpipes • ride horses • swim

a) **Complete[2] the sentences[3].**

1 On the Isle of Skye, they don't ___________.

2 At Loch Ness, they ___________.

3 At Dunrobin, they ___________.

b) **Which[4] place would you like to visit: the Isle of Skye, Loch Ness or Dunrobin? Tell your partner.**

*I would like to visit ...*

[1] tick *abhaken* [2] complete *ergänzen* [3] sentence *Satz* [4] which *welche(r,s)*

# Structuring[1] your ideas

The big surprise /
An exciting sea trip / ...

## 1 Choose a title[2]

You're going to write an adventure story.
First, choose a title and write it into the blue bubble of the mind map.

## 2 Answer the WH-questions

a) Answer these questions and complete[3] the mind map with words from the box.

**Ideas**
me • mum and dad • my little sister/brother • my class / friends • last summer • last holidays • Loch Ness • really big • Scotland • two weeks ago • suddenly, we saw something in the water • ...

- When did it happen?
- Who were you with?
- Where were you?
- What happened?

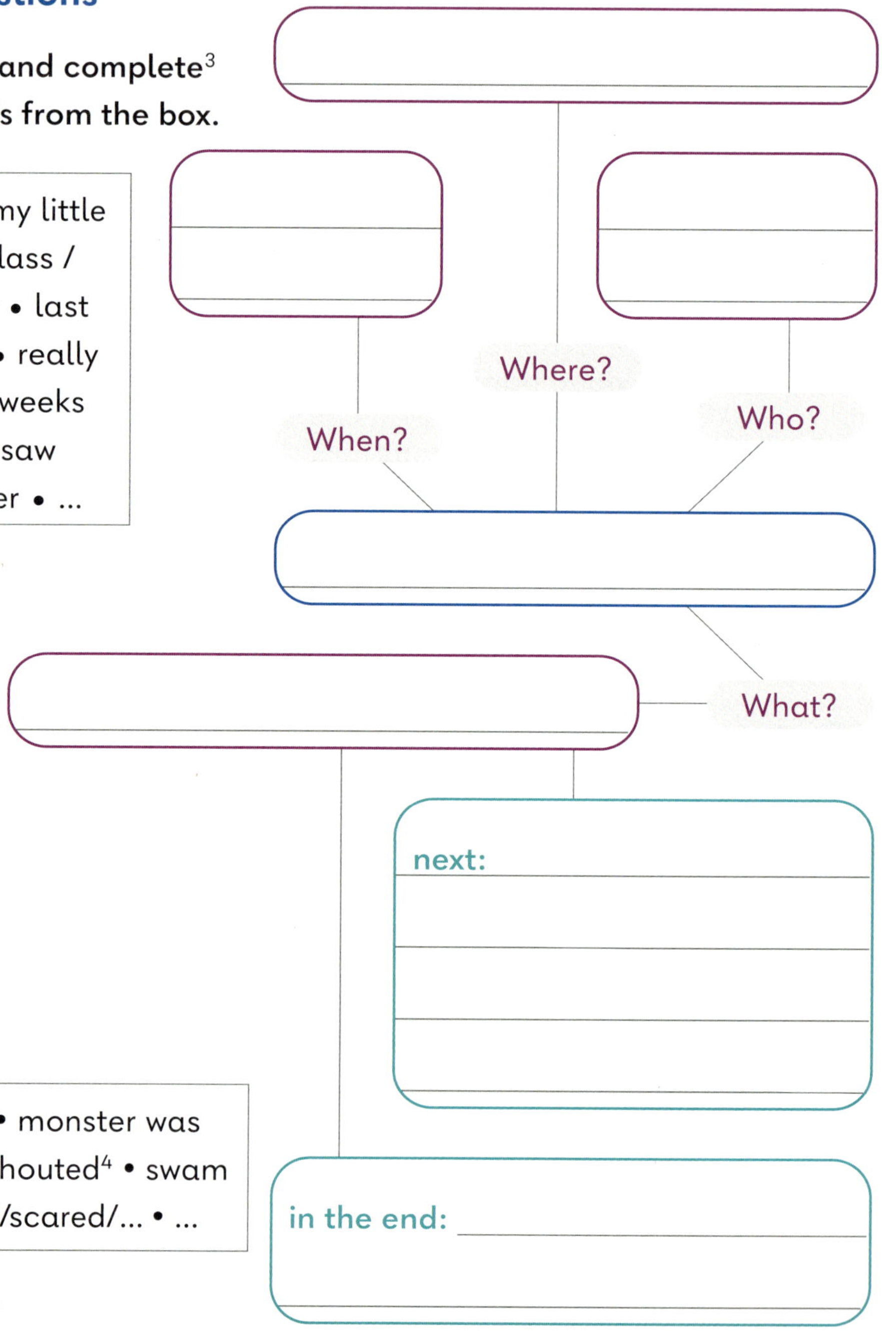


b) Think of more ideas. Answer these questions and complete the rest of the mind map with words from the box.

**Ideas**
everyone was scared • monster was scared too • someone shouted[4] • swam away • we felt excited/scared/... • ...

- What happened next?
- How did you feel in the end?

[1] **structure** *ordnen* [2] **title** *Titel, Überschrift* [3] **complete** *ergänzen* [4] **shout** *rufen, schreien*



Digital quiz Ich kann **Ideen für eine Geschichte ordnen.**

# Write a short adventure story

## Step[1] 1

▸ Digital help

Write your story. Use your mind map from page 88. Start with the first three WH-questions.

When? / Who? / Where? ______________________________

______________________________

______________________________

What? ______________________________

Next: ______________________________

______________________________

In the end: ______________________________

## Step 2

▸ Digital help

a) Read the checklist. Have you answered all the questions?

b) Write your story again in your exercise book.

**Checklist**

- Does it have a beginning[2], middle[3] and end?
- Have you used the simple past? (*saw, visited, went to*)
- Have you used linking words? (*and, but, because, so*)
- Have you spelled[4] everything correctly[5]? (~~schouted~~ – shouted)
- Have you used adjectives and adverbs? (it was a rainy afternoon, she shouted loudly)

## Step 3

Read your partner's story or listen as they read it out loud. Give feedback.

*You used linking words.*

*I like your story.*

*You used interesting adjectives.*

▸ Extra practice 8, p. 98

[1] **step** *Schritt* [2] **beginning** *Anfang* [3] **middle** *Mitte* [4] **spell** *buchstabieren* [5] **correctly** *richtig*

Digital quiz

Ich kann eine kurze Abenteuergeschichte schreiben.

## 1 Speaking A day in Edinburgh

Ich kann über Schottland reden.

**Look at the website. Say which[1] place you want to visit.**

www.discover-Edinburgh.example.net

**Edinburgh Castle**
The perfect place to find out about Scottish history. You can take amazing pictures of the city.

Ticket: £19.50
Child[2] ticket (age[3] 7–15): £11.40

**Edinburgh Zoo**
Our zoo[4] is home to over 2,500 animals from around the world.

Ticket: £24.25
Child ticket (age 3–15): £15.70

I want to go to ... • I want to learn about ... • I really like ... •
It's cheaper than ... • I don't want to go to ... • I think ... is boring • ...

## 2 Listening Grace's story

Ich kann Geschichten und Sagen verstehen *(adverbs of manner).*

a) **Listen to Grace's story.**
**What's the right picture? Circle[5] A or B.**

b) **Listen again. Circle.**

1 Culloden is a small village / big city.
2 Soldiers fought there almost 3 / 300 years ago.
3 The ghosts come back every year / day.
4 The ghosts come to Culloden on 1st / 16th April.

c) Language **Write adverbs.**

I went to Culloden last April – and I saw a ghost! He walked ____________ (1 slow) and ____________ (2 sad). I went back to my car ____________ (3 quiet) because I didn't want him to see me!

Check

[1] **which** *welche(r,s)* [2] **child** *Kind* [3] *age Alter* [4] **zoo** *Zoo* [5] **circle** *umkreisen*

## 3 The Adventure Centre's website

Ich kann über Aktivitäten und Abenteuer reden.

a) Language **Complete[1] the sentences[2] with *have, haven't, has* or *hasn't*.**

www.adventure-centre-who-is-who.example.net

Meet our two new instructors: Gemma and Ron.

Gemma is 25 and she's from Inverness.

She _________ (1) always loved adventure, but she _________ (2 not) ever jumped off a cliff before! Ron is 21. He's from Glasgow and this is his first job. We know that he'll be great! He _________ (3 not) been an instructor before, but he _________ (4) always spent time outdoors. For the last two weeks, we _________ (5) travelled with Gemma and Rob around this wonderful part of Scotland. It already feels like they _________ (6) been with us for a long time!

b) Words **Write the words.**

1 Have you ever jumped off a _ _ _ _ _ (cfilf) before? It's amazing!

2 Here is a full list of what things you need to _ _ _ _ (pcak).

3 You can do so many different _ _ _ _ _ _ _ (oootudr) activities with us.

4 You will be safe with us! Our instructors will _ _ _ _ _ _ _ (peotcrt) you.

[1] complete *ergänzen* [2] sentence *Satz*

Check

# United

## A magazine for young people across the UK

**Scottish traditions**[1] *by Rhona Murray*

### Hogmanay

*Hogmanay* is from 31 December to 2 January.
There are street parties, fireworks and lots of music!
In Stonehaven, Scotland, they have a very special *Hogmanay* celebration with fireballs[2]. It's amazing!
People sing the famous song *Auld Lang Syne*[3]. Robert Burns was a famous Scottish writer and he wrote the words.

*Auld Lang Syne*

Have you heard it before?

### Burns Night

Burns Night is on 25 January – the birthday of Robert Burns.
People get together and listen to bagpipes and read a special poem[4] by Robert Burns. Then they eat dinner – a special food called haggis: different parts of a sheep[5] mixed with oatmeal[6], onions and spices[7].
After dinner, people read more poems, play music and dance. At the end of the evening, everyone sings *Auld Lang Syne*.

Do you want to try haggis?

[1] tradition *Tradition* [2] fireball *Feuerball* [3] auld lang syne (Scots) = old long since *etwa: vor langer Zeit* [4] poem *Gedicht* [5] sheep *Schaf* [6] oatmeal *das Hafermehl* [7] spice *Gewürz*

## Let's dance!

This dance is called *Stripping the willow*[1].
Look at the pictures and watch a video online.

**Do you like to dance ?**

## Shortbread recipe

Have you ever tried shortbread? It's great and it's easy to make!
You need: 200g butter, 100g sugar, 300g flour.

Heat[2] the oven[3] to 160° C.

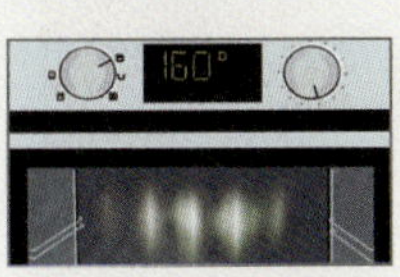


Put baking paper[4] in a tin[5].

Mix the butter and sugar.

Add[6] the flour and mix.

Press the shortbread into the tin.

Make small holes[7].

Bake for 25 minutes.

Cut the shortbread.

Enjoy!

[1] **Stripping the willow** *schottischer Tanz* [2] **heat** *vorheizen* [3] **oven** *Backofen*
[4] **baking paper** *Backpapier* [5] **tin** *Backblech* [6] **add** *hinzufügen* [7] **hole** *Loch*

# Partner page

## 1 The legend of the Loch Ness monster

▸ page 77

b) **Partner B: Read Grace's text on Nessie. Circle[1] A or B.**

A Scottish people don't like Nessie.

B There are lots of pictures of Nessie, but they aren't real.

**Nessie: The real story** *Grace*

Today we went to Loch Ness, a very big lake. It's famous because people think that Nessie, a monster, lives there. Every year lots of tourists spend money in the towns near the lake because they want to see Nessie.

But is Nessie real? There are many photos and videos of something in the water. But they aren't real!

There are lots of different animals and fish in the lake, but no monster.

I don't think that Nessie is real. But I still loved my visit to Loch Ness!

c) **Ask partner A these questions about Rhona's text.**

1 What happened in 1934?
2 Does Rhona think Nessie is real? Why or why not?

d) **Now answer partner A's questions.**

[1] **circle** *umkreisen*

# Extra practice

## Extra practice 1

▸ page 77

Find ten words from the story on page 77 in the box: →↓. Circle them.

| | | | | | | | | | | | | |
|---|---|---|---|---|---|---|---|---|---|---|---|---|
| T | | Z | | K | G | | C | A | S | T | L | E |
| O | G | M | F | O | H | G | X | F | T | M | | A |
| U | O | A | S | M | O | N | M | U | S | I | C | |
| R | B | P | P | | S | L | | | U | H | S | C |
| I | T | | | W | T | Q | V | E | H | I | B | |
| S | I | T | U | N | N | N | E | L | S | | U | C |
| T | M | A | | E | D | I | N | B | U | R | G | H |
| | E | L | | M | Q | X | S | O | R | N | K | Z |
| B | A | G | P | I | P | E | S | Y | T | | C | |

## Extra practice 2

▸ page 77

Complete[1] the sentences[2].

bagpipes • capital • castle • ghost • hiking •
kayaking • lake • legend • monster • tunnels

Last summer, I went to Scotland with my family. We visited Edinburgh first. That's the ________ (1) city of Scotland. Edinburgh is a really nice city with a big, old ________ (2). Lots of tourists visit the castle. There's a cool ________ (3) about a ghost. They say that this ________ (4) lives in the ________ (5) under the castle and plays the bagpipes, but we didn't hear ________ (6)!

Next, my dad wanted to go hiking, but my mum, my little brother and I don't like ________ (7). So we went ________ (8) on a ________ (9), but we didn't go to Loch Ness. My brother wanted to see the Loch Ness ________ (10). But ghosts and monsters aren't real!

[1] **complete** *ergänzen* [2] **sentence** *Satz*

## Extra practice 3

▶ page 77

a) Match[1] the blue words (adjectives) to the green words (adverbs). Draw lines[2].

| | |
|---|---|
| angry | well |
| careful | loudly |
| loud | happily |
| happy | quickly |
| quick | angrily |
| good | carefully |

b) Complete the sentences. Use the green words in a).

1 We saw the bus, so we ran ____________.

2 Class, please listen ____________.

3 Hafiz smiled ____________ at his new friend.

4 After the fight, Louisa closed the door ____________.

5 Do you sing ____________?

6 I really liked your story. You wrote it ____________.

c) Now write three sentences about yourself.

| | | |
|---|---|---|
| I | dance • do my homework • eat • read • run • talk • walk • write • ... | carefully • happily • loudly • proudly • quickly • quietly • sadly • slowly • ... |

____________________________________________

____________________________________________

____________________________________________

____________________________________________

[1] **match** *zuordnen* [2] **line** *Linie*

## Extra practice 4

▶ page 79

**Complete the sentences. Use *have* or *has*.**

1 Misty ________ ridden a pony.

2 Jonas and Emil ________ travelled to Italy.

3 Cody ________ tried skiing.

4 I ________ climbed a tree.

5 You ________ swum in the sea.

6 We ________ tried surfing.

## Extra practice 5

▶ page 85

**Write the words under the pictures.**

cliff • helicopter • map • sandwich • trainers • valley • walking boots • water bottle

 ________
 ________
 ________
 ________

 ________
 ________
 ________
 ________

## Extra practice 6

▶ page 85

Life skills **What should Rhona and Grace do next time? Tell each other.**

| | | | |
|---|---|---|---|
| Next time | Grace<br>Rhona | should | wear the right shoes. |
| | | | stay with the group. |
| | | shouldn't | ask her friend to do something dangerous. |

## Extra practice 7

▸ page 86

**Circle[1] the correct[2] linking word.**

1 I had plans to go hiking then / and I was so excited.

2 I put on a sweatshirt because / so it was cold.

3 It was sunny in the morning, because / but in the afternoon, it was cloudy.

4 I was very cold, so / because I walked quickly down the mountain.

5 After two hours I was at home and / then it was nice to be warm again.

6 I ate a really big pizza but / because I was so hungry!

## Extra practice 8

▸ page 89

**Look at the mind map and write a story.**

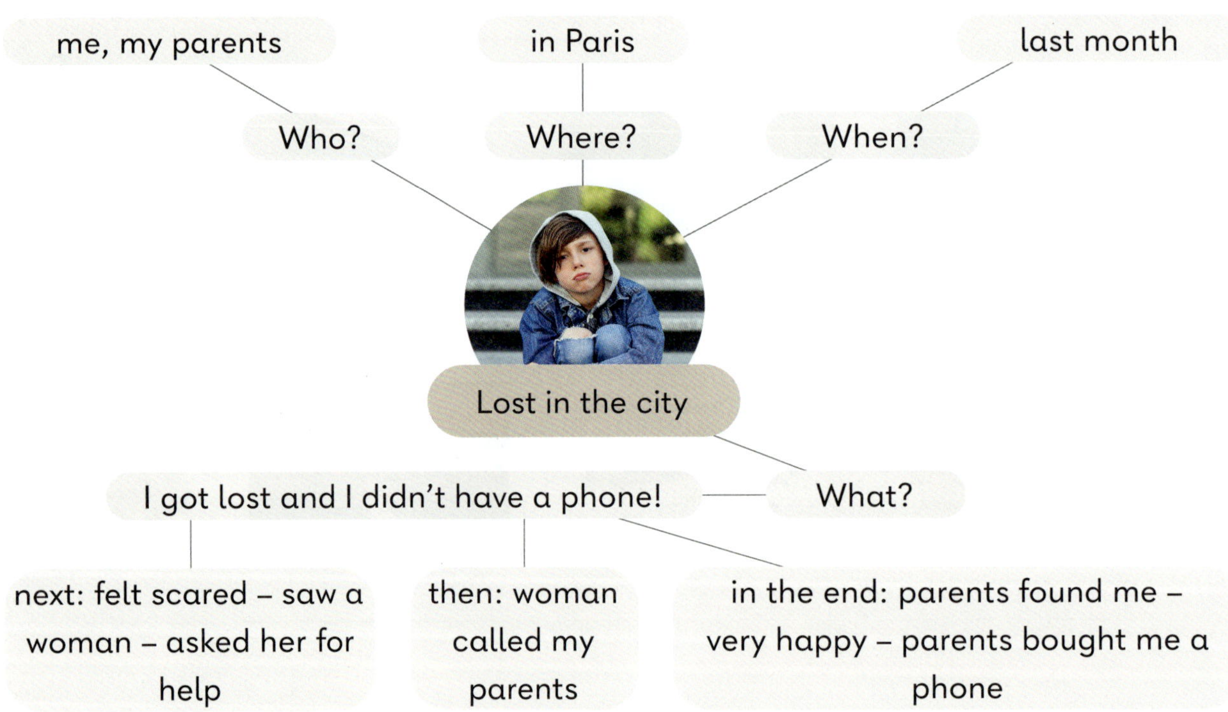


[1] circle *umkreisen* [2] correct *richtig*

## Unit 3
## Scotland: Adventure

| | | |
|---|---|---|
| ▸ p. 72 | **adventure** | das Abenteuer |
| | **capital (city)** | die Hauptstadt |
| | **kayaking** | das Kajakfahren |
| | **lake** | der See |
| | (to) **sound** | klingen *(sich … anhören)* |
| | **monster** | das Monster |
| ▸ p. 73 | (to) **hike** | wandern |
| | **high** | hoch |

kayaking

### Topic 1

| | | |
|---|---|---|
| ▸ p. 74 | **legend** | die Legende, die Sage |
| | **popular** | beliebt, populär |
| ▸ p. 76 | **Scottish** | schottisch |
| | **soldier** | der Soldat, die Soldatin |
| | (to) **find out (about)** | herausfinden; sich informieren (über) |
| | **around …** | um (… herum), in … umher |
| | (to) **carry** | tragen |
| | **safe(ly)** | sicher |
| ▸ p. 77 | **a long time ago** | vor langer Zeit |
| | **tunnel** | der Tunnel |
| | **no one** | niemand |
| | (to) **scare sb.** | jn. erschrecken, jm. Angst machen |
| | **quick(ly)** | schnell |

soldiers

### Topic 2

| | | |
|---|---|---|
| ▸ p. 78 | **outdoor activity** | die Outdoor-Aktivität; die Aktivität für draußen / im Freien |
| | **off** | weg von; hinunter von |
| | **cliff** | die Klippe |
| | (to) **ride a horse**, *simple past:* **rode**, *present perfect:* **ridden** | (ein Pferd / auf einem Pferd) reiten |
| | **tent** | das Zelt |
| | (to) **ski** | Ski laufen, Ski fahren |

**tents** on a **campsite**

| | | |
|---|---|---|
| | (to) **forget, forgot, forgotten** | vergessen |
| | **sleep: I've slept** | ich habe geschlafen |
| ▸ p. 79 | **go: I've gone** | ich bin gegangen |
| | **do: I've done** | ich habe getan |
| | **ready** | fertig, bereit |
| | (to) **pack** | packen, einpacken |
| | **bottle** | die Flasche |
| | **not ... yet** | noch nicht ... |
| | **put: I've put** | ich habe (*etwas wohin*) getan |
| ▸ p. 80 | **instructor** | der/die Lehrer/in, der/die Ausbilder/in |
| | **ever** | jemals, schon einmal |
| | **swim: I've swum** | ich bin geschwommen |
| | **hurt: I've hurt** | ich habe (*mich*) verletzt |
| ▸ p. 81 | (to) **be: I've been** | ich bin gewesen |
| | **try: I've tried** | ich habe versucht |

## Topic 3

| | | |
|---|---|---|
| ▸ p. 82 | (to) **protect** | schützen, beschützen |
| | **nature** | die Natur |
| | (to) **leave, left, left** | zurücklassen |
| | **path** | der Pfad |
| | **flower** | die Blume; die Blüte |
| ▸ p. 83 | (to) **recycle** | recyceln, wiederverwerten |
| | **air** | die Luft |

## Story

| | | |
|---|---|---|
| ▸ p. 84 | **trainer** | der Turnschuh |

a trainer

| | | |
|---|---|---|
| | (to) **put sth. on** | etwas anziehen |

| | | |
|---|---|---|
| ▶ p. 85 | **valley** | das Tal |
| | (to) **cry** | weinen |
| | (to) **breathe** | atmen |

There's a river in the **valley**.

| | |
|---|---|
| **helicopter** | der Hubschrauber |
| **as** | während |
| (to) **wait** | warten |
| **dangerous** | gefährlich |

a **helicopter**

## Study skills

| | | |
|---|---|---|
| ▶ p. 88 | (to) **shout** | rufen, schreien |

**Irregular verbs**

| **Infinitive** | **Simple past** | **Past participle** | |
|---|---|---|---|
| (to) **be** | **was/were** | **been** | sein |
| (to) **do** | **did** | **done** | tun |
| (to) **forget** | **forgot** | **forgotten** | vergessen |
| (to) **go** | **went** | **gone** | gehen |
| (to) **hurt** | **hurt** | **hurt** | schmerzen, wehtun |
| (to) **leave** | **left** | **left** | verlassen |
| (to) **put** | **put** | **put** | legen, stellen |
| (to) **read** | **read** | **read** | lesen |
| (to) **ride** | **rode** | **ridden** | reiten; (Rad) fahren |
| (to) **sleep** | **slept** | **slept** | schlafen |
| (to) **spend** | **spent** | **spent** | (Geld) ausgeben, (Zeit) verbringen |
| (to) **swim** | **swam** | **swum** | schwimmen |

# Unit 4
# Wales: Digital life

A

Donkeys on Llandudno beach

B

Wales uses green energy.

C

Our national sport

D

There are more sheep than people in Wales!

## 1 Reading **An online quiz about Wales**

a) Before you read **Dylan and Owen have made a website about Wales. Look at the pictures. What do you see? Tell each other.**

*I can see a beach and ...*

*There's a road and ...*

b) **Dylan and Owen have made a quiz. It's on** page 103**. Can you guess[1] the answers? Circle[2].**

c) **Compare[3] your answers with your partner.**

---

[1] **guess** *raten* [2] **circle** *umkreisen* [3] **compare** *vergleichen*

**Nach dieser Unit kann ich ...**

- ◯ ein Quiz über Wales durchführen
- ◯ über Wales sprechen
- ◯ einfache Anleitungen geben
- ◯ über soziale Medien sprechen
- ◯ flüssig vortragen

**Unit task**

- ◯ einen kurzen Vortrag über soziale Medien halten

### Dylan and Owen's quiz about Wales

1 In Wales, people speak ...
A English and Welsh
B English and Scottish

2 Look at this map. What colour is Wales?
A blue
B yellow

3 Llandudno is the name for ...
A a pet donkey
B our town

4 What is on the Welsh flag?
A a red dragon
B a red cat

5 What is national sport in Wales?
A rugby
B judo

6 There are three million people in Wales. How many million sheep are there?
A one million sheep
B ten million sheep

## 2 Listening **Dylan and Owen's message**

a) Listen. Check your answers from 1b).

b) Read these sentences[1], then listen again. Write true (T) or false[2] (F)?

1 Dylan and Owen are in class 8A. ☐
2 Owen speaks Welsh at home. ☐
3 Dylan and Owen play rugby. ☐
4 Dylan loves to use social media. ☐

c) What places near you can you show other people? Check Wordbank 8, page 147.

▸ Wordbank 8, p. 147

[1] sentence *Satz* [2] false *falsch*

Digital quiz **Ich kann Informationen über Wales verstehen.** ✓

# Welcome to Wales

**Good to know**

Wales has one of the longest place names in the world.

Listen.

## 1 Reading **Talking about the class videos**

**Read. Which[1] place do you want to visit?**

**Gwen** ___ My video is finished! 😊 I'm really happy with mine. What about your video, Flynn? Where have you filmed yours?

**Flynn** ___ At the ski centre. Promit has already finished his video. He made his about GreenWood adventure park.

**Dylan** ___ Cool! Owen and I have almost finished our video.

**Owen** ___ Yeah, Dylan is writing a song for ours. 😊

**Gwen** ___ Samara and Louise have just finished their video. They filmed the beach in Llandudno. I think theirs will be popular because of the donkeys.

## 2 Looking at language **Mine and yours**

a) **Complete[2] the table with the blue possessive pronouns in 1.**

| I | you | he | she | it | we | they |
|---|---|---|---|---|---|---|
| my (video) | your (video) | his (video) | her (video) | its (video) | our (video) | their (video) |
| ______ | ______ | ______ | *hers* | *its* | ______ | ______ |

b) **Complete 1–4 with possessive pronouns from the table.**

**Flynn** ___ Megan sent me her video. *Hers* ______ (1) is my favourite video!

**Gwen** ___ I think all our videos are amazing.

**Flynn** ___ I've almost finished my video. I'm happy that I chose the ski centre for ______ (2).

**Gwen** ___ Can I help you with your video? What do you still need for ______ (3)?

**Flynn** ___ I'm trying to find the right music for it. Have you heard the song for Dylan and Owen's video? I think ______ (4) is going to be so good!

► Extra practice 1–2, p. 123

[1] **which** *welche(r, s)* [2] **complete** *ergänzen*

## 3 Song Dylan's song

a) Before you listen **What do you think Dylan will say about Wales in his song *Cymru*? Circle[1], then tell each other.**

1 Wales is boring.
2 Wales is a mixture of old and new.
3 The old parts are the best.

*Cymru* (Wales auf Walisisch)

Du findest den Liedtext auf Seite 124, Extra practice 3.

b) **Listen to the song. Were you right?**

c) **What do you think about the song?**

*I like the music / text / ...*
*It makes me feel ...*

▸ Wordbank 4, p. 143

### My task

## 4 Record[2] a voice message[3]

a) **Record a voice message for Dylan. Tell him what you want to do in Wales. First write your message. You can start like this:** *Hi Dylan, I can't wait for the trip! It's going to be so much fun. Here's what I want to do in Wales.*

▸ Digital help

| | | |
|---|---|---|
| I really want to | visit | an adventure park • the beach • a castle • Cardiff • ... |
| I would like to | go | shopping • hiking • swimming • on a tour • ... |
| Also, can we | buy | a toy dragon • a hat • a T-shirt • some chocolate • ... |

b) **Now record your message for Dylan.**

[1] **circle** *umkreisen* [2] **record** *aufnehmen* [3] **voice message** *Sprachnachricht*

Digital quiz Ich kann über Wales sprechen.

# Life with and without technology[1]

## 1 Viewing **Life in a Welsh village in 1927**

A

B

C

D

**a)** Before you watch **How did people live in a Welsh village in 1927? What do you think are the right answers? Circle[2] A or B.**

1 What did they wear? A Clothes they bought online. B Clothes they made.

2 How did they travel? A People walked a lot. B Everyone drove cars.

3 What did they do for fun? A They sang. B They watched TV.

**b) Watch part 1 of the video and answer the questions.**

1 Why do the people in the video want to live in the past? *It's for a* ______________.
2 What does the boy miss the most? *He misses* ______________.

**c) Now watch all the video (parts 1 and 2). What would you miss the most?**

I would miss ________________________________________ the most.

**d) Does technology bring people together? Tick[3] (✓) what you agree with.**

*Yes, it does, because ...*

A you can talk to family. ☐

B you can make new friends. ☐

*No, it doesn't, because ...*

A it's easy to be mean to people. ☐

B people spend too much time online. ☐

[1] **technology** *Technologie* [2] **circle** *umkreisen* [3] **tick** *abhaken*

## 2 A letter from 1927

**Read this letter. Complete[1] the sentences[2] with the *simple past*. Why did Jonathon go to Cardiff? Circle.**

A To buy a car. B To get medicine.
C For a job.

**Remember**

Mit dem *simple past* sprichst du über Dinge, die in der Vergangenheit geschehen sind. Auf den Seiten 138–139 findest du die unregelmäßigen Verben im *simple past*.

*Dear Mother,*
*It is evening here in Cardiff. Everyone else is already asleep, but I want to write you a letter. We* arrived *(1 arrive) in Cardiff two days ago. It* was *(2 be) a hard journey because we* didn't stop *(3 not stop) all day. We ______ (4 be) very tired, but we ______ (5 know) that we ______ (6 have) to get here fast. We ______ (7 ask) to see the doctor right away, but he ______ (8 not have) time until yesterday because he is so busy. Many people in Cardiff are ill too. But he ______ (9 say) that he can give us the medicine on Friday.*
*I hope that it will help father. I'll write again soon. Jonathon*

▸ Extra practice 4, p. 124

## 3 Speaking An evening with or without technology?

a) **What did you do yesterday evening? Write three sentences in your exercise book.**

| | | |
|---|---|---|
| Yesterday evening | I<br>my family and I<br>my friends and I | did homework / …<br>went shopping / to a friend's house / …<br>listened to music / …<br>played football / basketball / …<br>watched videos on social media / a film / … |

b) Walk around **Tell different partners what you did. Ask your partners what they did. How many students used technology or social media?**

*What did you do?*

*Yesterday evening I …*

[1] **complete** *ergänzen* [2] **sentence** *Satz*

## 4 On the phone

a) Read. Complete the phone call[1] with the words in the box.

after • problem • say • sorry • tomorrow • yesterday

**Owen** Hi Dylan. How are things? What did you do ______________ (1)?

**Dylan** Great, thanks. I watched a video about life in 1927. It was interesting – I'll send you the link.

**Owen** Oh yes – videos. We still need to finish ours. Are you free later after dinner?

**Dylan** No, ______________ (2), I have to help my mum with her new smartwatch. What about tomorrow?

**Owen** What? Sorry, I can't hear you.

**Dylan** Can you hear me now? I said: Let's finish our video ______________ (3).

**Owen** Yeah, that's cool. How about at your house after school?

**Dylan** What? Can you ______________ (4) that again, please?

**Owen** How about at your house ______________ (5) school?

**Dylan** Yes, that's fine[2].

**Owen** Oh, one more thing, Dylan. Can we use your computer? Mine is broken.

**Dylan** Sure, no ______________ (6). Sorry, I have to go now ...

b) Listen and check.

## 5 Words Instructions

**Match the pictures (A–D) to the instructions (1–4).**

1 charge the phone ☐

2 tap to open the app ☐

3 download the app ☐

4 switch off and switch on the phone ☐

A 

B 

C 

D 

▸ Wordbank 9, p. 148

[1] **phone call** *Telefongespräch*

## 6 Mediation **Explaining instructions**

a) Partner B: Look at page 122.
Partner A: Your parent (partner B) needs help with a new smartwatch.
Complete instructions 1–4 in German.
Then tell partner B what to do.

1 *First, charge your smartwatch.*
2 *Go to 'Settings' on your phone.*
3 *Check that Bluetooth is on.*
4 *Next, download the app on your phone.*

1 Zuerst musst du die Uhr ____________.

2 ________________________________________________ zu Einstellungen.

3 ______________________________________________________________

4 ______________________________________________________________

b) Now you're the parent. Listen to partner B's instructions.

### My task

## 7 Commands[1] for a digital assistant[2]

a) Read these commands for a digital assistant. Agree on the top three most useful commands with a partner. Tick (✓) them.

- Switch on the lights. ☐
- Play a song. ☐
- Tell me what the weather is like today. ☐
- Switch on the TV. ☐
- Tell me a joke. ☐
- Say something in a different language. ☐

b) Partner A: Now you're the digital assistant. Act out your partner's commands.
Partner B: Give your digital assistant commands.

*Paula, tell me what the weather is like today!*

*It's sunny and warm today.*

[1] **command** *Befehl, Kommando* [2] **assistant** *der Assistent, die Assistentin*

Digital quiz Ich kann **einfache Anleitungen geben.**

# Social media

## 1 Listening Online life

a) Before you listen **Find out: What are the most popular social media apps in your class?**

*I use ... What about you?*

*I really like ...*

b) **Listen. Do the people think social media is good (☺), bad (☹) or good and bad (☺ ☹)? Draw emojis.**

1 Samara ___ 2 Promit ___ 3 Gwen ___ 4 Flynn ___

c) **What's the right order? Listen again and write 1–4.**

A I followed some people online. 1

B It feels good when I get a lot of likes. ☐

C I use an app that helps me. ☐

D It's hard to delete photos or videos. ☐

▶ Extra practice 5, p. 125

## 2 Life skills Can an app make people feel better?

a) **Listen and complete[1] the sentences[2]. Circle[3] A or B.**

1 Flynn uses the app when he
A has a problem. B is hungry.

2 Or when he's angry or
A worried. B happy.

3 He writes down his thoughts[4] and
A recipes. B feelings.

b) **What can you do when you have a problem? Circle one. Can you think of one more? Tell your partner.**

draw or sing • go for a walk • hit[5] a cushion • hug my pet • talk to a friend • talk to a teacher • talk to parents • ...

[1] **complete** *ergänzen* [2] **sentence** *Satz* [3] **circle** *umkreisen* [4] **thought** *Gedanke* [5] **hit** *schlagen*

## 3 Speaking **Could you help me, please?**

a) Read or listen.
Then complete the sentence.

______________ is helping

______________ to make an account.

b) Walk around What can you help someone with? What do you need help with? Circle the words in the box and talk with different partners.

*Could you help me with …?*

*I can help you with …*

| |
|---|
| homework • a computer problem • an email • an app • drawing • singing • dancing • … |

**Owen** I want to try the Zenn app, but I don't know where to start.
**Dylan** I can help you if you like.
**Owen** Yes, please. Could you please help me to make an account?
**Dylan** No problem. You need a profile photo. Shall I upload one for you, or do you want to do it?
**Owen** Can you do it, please? Look, this one is good.
**Dylan** Sure. There you go. Your account is private. Would you like me to make it public?
**Owen** No, thanks. And what should I put in my bio?
**Dylan** Just some information about yourself and maybe a few emojis.

## 4 Writing **A bio**

a) Match the emojis (A–D) to Owen's bio.

| | | |
|---|---|---|
| A |  | my music |
| B |  | my birthday |
| C |  | my friends |
| D |  | my home |

OwenT (✓)
- 1 12th June
- 2 Llandudno
- 3 Dylan, Samara and Flynn
- 4 pop, rock, rap – everything!

b) Write your own bio.

______________________ your picture

1 ______________________

2 ______________________

3 ______________________

4 ______________________

## 5 Reading **Fact and opinion**

a) Before you read **What social media do you get news or information from?**

b) **Read the texts.**

A

www.example.com/llandudno-times

**Cyberbullying is a big problem**
The charity *Ditch the label* has researched how teenagers use social media. The people that work for *Ditch the label* have found a big problem: One in five teenagers has experienced bullying online. Many of them did not say anything about the messages that they got. More people are using social media, so the problem is getting bigger. But there is good news: 58% of teenagers who became victims of bullying said their teachers helped them with the problem.

B

SOCIAL MEDIA IS TERRIBLE!!!
We have to stop social media! Everyone who uses it is a bully! Some boys who go to my daughter's school sent horrible messages to her. It happens to everyone, my daughter says. The person that made social media wanted all teens to fight each other. Social media is terrible!!!

*Datenquelleen zu A: cybercrew.uk und mayoclinic.org (siehe Quellenverzeichnis)*

c) **Match[1] the sentences to text A or B in b).**

1 It only talks about the writer's opinions. ☐

2 It talks about research[2]. ☐

## 6 Looking at language **Relative clauses**

Erklär-film

**Read examples 1–3. They are from text A in 5b). Complete the rules in the box.**

1 The people that work for *Stop Bullies* ...

2 the messages that they got ...

3 58 % of teenagers who became victims of bullying ...

Mit Relativsätzen *(relative clauses)* gibst du zusätzliche Informationen über Personen oder Dinge.

Für Personen verwendest du ________ oder ________.

Für Dinge verwendest du nur ________.

[1] **match** *zuordnen* [2] **research** *Recherche, Forschung*

## 7 What is it?

a) Draw lines.

| | |
|---|---|
| 1 Social media is something ... | A that is true. |
| 2 An influencer is a person ... | B who subscribes to your page or channel. |
| 3 A follower is someone ... | C who has lots of followers on social media. |
| 4 A fact is information ... | D that you use to talk to people online. |

b) Complete the sentences with *who* or *that*.

1 A bio is a text ______________ explains all about you on social media.

2 A bully is someone ______________ is mean to other people.

3 A victim is someone ______________ experiences bullying.

▸ Extra practice 6–7, p. 125–126

### My task

## 8 The debate[1]

a) Help Dylan and Owen with the debate.
Partner B: Go to page 122.
Partner A: Why is social media a good thing for teens? Complete the sentences.

▸ Digital help

you can talk to friends/family • it's fun to follow people • it feels good to get lots of likes • ...

Social media is a good thing for teens because ______________________________.

Also, ____________________________________________.

I think that ______________________________________.

b) Check your writing. Then read your partner's sentences. Give feedback.

[1] debate *Debatte*

igital quiz Ich kann über gute und schlechte Seiten der sozialen Medien sprechen.

# Looking good

## 1 Reading The camera never lies[1], right?

> *Skimming* bedeutet, dass du einen Text nur überfliegst, um zu wissen, um was es geht.

**a)** Before you read **Skim the story. Circle[2] A, B or C in 1 and 2.**

1 I think that Dylan is going to ...
A buy a new car. B edit[3] his pictures. C be mean to Owen.

2 I think that Owen is going to ...
A laugh at Dylan. B edit his pictures. C get annoyed[4].

**b)** **Now read the story. Were your ideas in a) right?**

### Are Dylan's posts real?

'Thanks for helping me with my bio, Dylan!' said Owen. 'I like to use social media now!' 'You're welcome!' said Dylan. 'I like that we can talk to our German exchange partners. My partner Saskia is sooo cool!' Later, Owen saw a new post from Dylan.

'Dylan's family doesn't have a new car,' he thought. 'He has edited that photo.' The next day at school, Dylan was really excited. 'You know that new photo I posted? It got so many likes!'

At the weekend, Owen and Dylan went to the beach. Dylan just wanted to take photos.

'This is boring!' said Owen. 'Let's go swimming now.' 'Just one more photo,' said Dylan. 'The light is really good now. And I've got lots of followers who need to see how cool I look.' 'You mean you want Saskia to see how cool you look,' said Owen.

### Owen gets annoyed

On Monday, Owen saw a new photo of Dylan. 'I took that photo of him last weekend, but he's edited it!' Owen thought. He was annoyed.

[1] **lie** *lügen* [2] **circle** *umkreisen* [3] **edit** *bearbeiten, editieren* [4] **get annoyed** *sich ärgern*

Later, the German exchange students arrived. Dylan finally met Saskia.

'It's great to meet you, Saskia!' he said.

'Hi, Dylan?' Saskia said. 'You look different in your photos.' 'Er ... well, it's me,' said Dylan. Owen watched them and felt annoyed again.

**Owen wants to do something BIG**

That evening, Owen looked at Dylan's photos again and again.

'He thinks he's so cool. I'm going to show everyone how cool he really is,' he thought. He posted a photo of Dylan. In this photo, Dylan didn't look great.

People wrote mean things under the photo. They made jokes about Dylan and said he looked horrible. At first Owen thought it was funny ... but later he felt bad and deleted the photo.

**Saying sorry**

The next day, Owen saw Dylan and Saskia in the canteen. Dylan looked unhappy. Owen sat down next to them. 'I'm really sorry about the photo, Dylan,' said Owen. 'That was really mean of me.'
'Hi Owen,' said Dylan. 'It was mean. And at first I was really angry. But then I thought about it. It was also weird of me to post things that weren't real. I wanted to get a lot of likes.'

Saskia turned and smiled at Dylan. 'You know, I think you look better in Owen's photo. It's real.' Dylan smiled back at Saskia. He felt better. 'I guess followers and likes aren't important,' he said.

## 2 What happened in the story?

Are the sentences[1] true (T) or false[2] (F)?

1 Owen doesn't use social media. ☐

2 Dylan edits his pictures. ☐

3 Dylan's family has a new car. ☐

4 It was mean of Owen to post that photo. ☐

## 3 Double circle Social media opinions

Look at the questions. Answer them for yourself. Then talk to a partner and ask question 1. Ask new partners questions 2–4.

| | |
|---|---|
| 1 Do you use social media? | I often / sometimes / never use social media. |
| 2 Which influencers do you know? | ________ is a famous influencer. |
| 3 Is it a good idea to edit photos to make them look better? | I think it is / isn't a good idea to edit photos. |
| 4 How do you feel when you see photos of people who look perfect? | When I see these photos, I feel bad / sad / happy. |

## 4 Life skills Recognizing[3] fake photos

a) Influencers use different tools to make themselves look good.
Which of these tools (A–F) have you used? Tick[4] (✓) them.

A filters ☐ B lighting ☐ C digital editing software ☐

D poses ☐ E clothes ☐ F make-up ☐

b) Look at the left photo of Dylan on page 115. Which tools in 4a) do you think he used in the photo? Circle them in a).

[1] sentence *Satz* [2] false *falsch* [3] recognize *erkennen* [4] tick *abhaken*

Digital quiz Ich kann über Wahres und Unwahres in den sozialen Medien sprechen.

# Sophie's cosplay costume

**Good to know**

*Cosplay* ist ein Hobby. Fans verkleiden sich wie Charaktere aus Videospielen oder Filmen und verhalten sich auch so. Sie posten Bilder und Videos von sich online, treffen sich auf Veranstaltungen oder nehmen an Wettbewerben teil.

## 1 Before you watch **Cosplay**

**Which character would you choose to cosplay and why? Tell your partner.**

*I'd choose Wonder Woman / … because she's strong / cool …*

## 2 Viewing **Sophie's costume**

**Sophie is a German vlogger. Watch the first part of the video. Draw lines[1].**

| | |
|---|---|
| 1 Who made the costume? | A She forgot to make a video. |
| 2 How long did the costume take? | B Sophie. |
| 3 Why did she make the costume? | C Two weeks. |
| 4 What was the problem in Stuttgart? | D To learn new things. |

▸ Extra practice 8, p. 126

## 3 Viewing **In Cologne[2]**

**Watch the next part of the video. True (T) or false[3] (F)?**

1 People didn't look at Sophie. ☐
2 Sophie made a video. ☐
3 She won a costume competition. ☐
4 It was a great experience. ☐

## 4 Life skills **Don't give up[4]!**

**You are unhappy with a project[5]. Read the questions. Circle[6] the best answers for you.**

1 How do you feel? A Great. B Bored. C Happy. D Angry. E Sad.
2 What can you do? A Give up. B Take a break. C Try again. D Ask for help.

[1] **line** *Linie* [2] **Cologne** *Köln* [3] **false** *falsch* [4] **give up** *aufgeben* [5] **project** *Projekt*
[6] **circle** *umkreisen*

# Make a talk flow[1]

Sammle zuerst Ideen für deinen Vortrag und ordne sie.

- Mache dir Karten mit kurzen Notizen (Keywords und Tipps).

## 1 Order ideas

a) Saskia is giving a talk about social media. Look at her cards[2]. What is the right order? Write 1–4.

__ **What I do online**
– chat with friends
– upload photos and videos
– account is private

1 **Intro**
Say:
1 What I do online
2 Social media: ☺ & ☹

__ **End**
Say:
Thank you
Ask:
Questions?

__ **Social media: ☺ & ☹:**
☺ friends, vloggers
☹ posts aren't real, people can be mean

b) Now listen to Saskia's talk. Were you right in a)?

## 2 Explain words

Saskia has forgotten the word *habit*. How can she explain it? Circle[3] A or B.

A Something that you do often.
B Something that you never do.

*I can't find the word I'm looking for. ... Oh, I think it's 'habit', right?*

## 3 Keep talking!

When you need a minute to think, you can use these phrases[4]:

A You know, ... • B Let me see, ... • C I mean, ... • D Just a minute, ... • E Well, ...

Listen to Saskia's talk again. Which phrases does she use? Circle them.

[1] **flow** *fließend* [2] **card** *Karte* [3] **circle** *umkreisen* [4] **phrase** *Redewendung*



Digital quiz Ich kann einen Vortrag flüssig präsentieren.

# Give a short talk about social media

## Step[1] 1

**You're going to give a short talk (two to three minutes) about your online and social media habits. Answer the questions with short notes.**

1 What do you do online? ______________________________

2 What are your favourite apps? ______________________________

3 What do you think is good or bad about social media? Exercise 8 on page 113 can help you.

▶ Digital help

______________________________

______________________________

## Step 2

**Make cards[2] with your ideas. Exercise 1 on page 118 can help you.**

## Step 3

**Find pictures for your talk. Make slides or print out[3] pictures that you can show.**

Achte darauf, dass die Verwendung der Bilder erlaubt ist.

## Step 4

**Practise your talk silently.**
**You can use a phone to record[4] yourself.**

## Step 5

**Give your talk to a group. The others listen. Your group gives feedback about:**

1 one good thing about the talk.
2 one thing that could be better.
3 one question.

*I liked your pictures.*

*Next time, you should talk more slowly.*

*How often do you use social media?*

[1] **step** *Schritt* [2] **card** *(Notiz-)Karte* [3] **print out** *ausdrucken* [4] **record** *aufnehmen*

Digital quiz

**Ich kann einen kurzen Vortrag halten.**

## 1 Reading A poster about Wales

Ich kann Informationen über Wales verstehen.

a) Skim[1] the texts and look at the photos. Circle[2] the best title[3] (A, B or C).

A Three free places to visit in Wales
B Three cool places for history fans
C The three best places for kids in Wales

### Conwy Castle

This castle is over 700 years old. It has eight towers. A family ticket costs £37.70. In summer it's open until 6 in the evening. It's a good idea to bring something to eat because there isn't a cafe in the castle.

### Penrhyn Castle

This castle is only about 200 years old and has a beautiful garden. There are two cafes, shops and a train museum. A family ticket costs £35 and the castle is open from 10 in the morning to 4 in the afternoon in summer.

### Castell Dinas Brân

You can't drive up to this castle – you can only walk there. It's high on a mountain. The castle is almost 800 years old. You'll need walking boots and a jacket because it's usually windy. You don't have to pay to visit this castle, but there are no shops, cafes or toilets.

b) Are the sentences[4] true (T) or false[5] (F)?

1 You can only walk to Castell Dinas Brân. ☐
2 All the castles have a cafe. ☐
3 Penrhyn Castle has a garden. ☐
4 Conwy Castle is the cheapest for families. ☐
5 Two castles are over 700 years old. ☐
6 Go to Conwy Castle if you like trains. ☐

[1] **skim** *einen Text überfliegen* [2] **circle** *umkreisen* [3] **title** *Titel* [4] **sentence** *Satz* [5] **false** *falsch*

Check

## 2 Words **Helping a neighbour**

Ich kann einfache Anleitungen geben. ✓

**Your neighbour doesn't speak German. Help him take a photo and send it to his daughter. (Circle) the right blue words.**

1 Open / Edit the camera app and take a photo.

2 Write / Open your messaging app.

3 Edit / Tap 'write new message'.

4 Tap / Edit the plus (+) and find your daughter's number.

5 Charge / Tap the camera.

6 Swipe / Tap the photo that you want to send.

7 Write / Open your message.

8 Tap / Edit 'send'. Finished! 😊

## 3 Language **Life online – positive or negative?**

Ich kann über gute und schlechte Seiten der sozialen Medien sprechen. ✓

a) **Complete[1] the sentences with *that/who*. Look at the blue words.**

1 Cyberbullying is a problem *that* ______ many people have experienced. ☹

2 People ______ can't walk can use social media to talk with friends. ☐

3 Shops ______ use social media can sell more products. ☐

4 Teenagers ______ use social media find friends with the same interests. ☐

5 There are lots of news stories on social media ______ are not true. ☐

6 If you use social media, you can find friends ______ live in different countries. ☐

b) **Which sentences are positive? Which are negative? Draw emojis in the boxes (☺ or ☹) in a).**

[1] **complete** *ergänzen*

Check

# Partner page

▶ page 109

## 6 Mediation Explaining instructions[1]

a) Partner B: You are a parent and you need help with a new smartwatch. Listen to partner A's instructions.

b) Now partner A is the parent. Complete[2] instructions 5–8 in German, then tell partner A what to do.

| |
|---|
| 5 Switch the smartwatch on. |
| 6 Next, choose a language on the watch. |
| 7 After that, tap the name of the watch on your phone. |
| 8 Finally, tap 'pair[3]' on your phone. |

5 Schalte ______________________________ .

6 Wähle ______________________________ .

7 ______________________________

8 ______________________________

▶ page 113

## 8 My task The debate[4]

a) Help Dylan and Owen with the debate. Partner B: Why is social media a bad thing for teens? Complete the sentences[5].

| |
|---|
| it is hard to delete things online • it can be dangerous • sometimes people are mean • … |

I believe that social media is a bad thing for teens because ______________ .

I think one of the problems with social media is that ______________ .

I think that ______________________________ .

b) Check your writing. Then read your partner's sentences. Give feedback.

[1] **instruction** *Anweisung* [2] **complete** *ergänzen* [3] **pair** *verkoppeln, verbinden* [4] **debate** *Debatte* [5] **sentence** *Satz*

# Extra practice

## Extra practice 1

▸ page 104

Look at the table. Complete it with the words in the box.

hers • his • mine • ours • theirs • yours

| | | |
|---|---|---|
| I | ______ | *meiner, meine, meins* |
| you | *yours* | *deiner, deine, deins; Ihrer, Ihre, Ihres* |
| he | ______ | *seiner, seine, seins* |
| she | ______ | *ihrer, ihre, ihres* |
| it | *its* | *seiner, seine, seins; ihrer, ihre, ihres* |
| we | ______ | *unserer, unsere, unseres* |
| you | ______ | *eurer, eure, eueres; Ihrer, Ihre, Ihres* |
| they | ______ | *ihrer, ihre, ihres* |

## Extra practice 2

▸ page 104

Complete the conversation. Circle[1] the correct[2] blue word.

**Mr Price** Somebody has forgotten their phone. It's on the desk over there. Owen, is it (yours) / hers (1) ?

**Owen** No, I've got his / mine (2) here.

**Dylan** Promit has a black phone, I think. Maybe it's his / theirs (4) .

**Louise** No, Promit and I have the same kind of phone – yours / ours (5) are smaller.

**Mr Price** Well, I'll look at the screen photo to see if that helps ... Oh, that's a picture of my family. Oops! It's his / mine (6)! Sorry!

[1] **circle** *umkreisen* [2] **correct** *korrekt*

## Extra practice 3

▸ page 105

### Cymru*

*Drop the beat, turn up the bass.*
*Let me tell you about a special place,*
*where everybody has the space to*
*breathe.*

*My Cymru where the fields are green,*
*the music's cool, the air is clean.*
*I love it and I never mean to leave.*

*Come see where the old meets new,*
*and the valleys meet the sea.*
*Come with me to my beautiful Cymru.*

*Mae hen wlad fy nhadau yn annwyl i*
*mi.*
*O dwi'n dy garu di fy Nghymru i!***

*We've got tech and the Brecon Beacons,*
*beautiful in every season.*
*That's why my Cymru cannot be beaten.*

*From the music clubs of Cardiff*
*to the hills of Aberystwyth –*
*everybody sing: Cymru am byth!****

* *Wales*
** *The land of my fathers is dear to me.*
*Oh I love you, my Wales!*
*** *Wales forever!*

## Extra practice 4

▸ page 107

**Complete[1] the sentences[2]. Use the simple past.**

What was ______ (1 be) life like for kids in the past?

A long time ago, most kids in the UK didn't go ______ (2 not go) to school because they ______ (3 have) to work. Also in Wales, many kids ______ (4 have) to work hard. They ______ (5 do) different kinds of jobs. They ______ (6 not have) many breaks and they ______ (7 not see) the sun[3] all day because they ______ (8 have) to work long days.

Today kids don't work there – they go to learn about the past and be tourists!

[1] **complete** *ergänzen* [2] **sentence** *Satz* [3] **sun** *Sonne*

## Extra practice 5

▶ page 110

**Dylan is telling Owen how he uses social media. Circle[1] the right word.**

My mum's family lives in Kenya, so it's nice to see what they're doing. We often watch / send (1) messages to each other, and my cousins always post / subscribe (2) photos of themselves. I really like to leave / watch (3) the videos that my uncle posts of his life in Nairobi. In fact, you should send / subscribe (4) to his channel, because the videos are really cool. He always gets / posts (5) a lot of likes, sometimes more than a thousand!

Nairobi, Kenia

## Extra practice 6

▶ page 113

**Partner A: Choose one of the pictures and tell partner B about it – but don't say what it is! Partner B: Guess what it is.**
**Swap roles[2] and choose another picture.**

| | |
|---|---|
| This is a thing that you can use to | go online • call people • check the time • listen to music • ... |
| This is a person who | makes websites / apps / games • takes a lot of photos / videos • plays video games for lots of people • ... |

A

B

C

D

E

F

[1] circle *umkreisen* [2] role *Rolle*

## Extra practice 7

▸ page 113

a) Complete[1] the sentences[2] with *who* or *that*.

1 This is an animal *that* you often see in Wales. ______

2 This is a symbol[3] of a country ______ is important to many people. ______

3 This is a language ______ people speak in Wales. ______

4 This is a person ______ can help you when you're ill. ______

5 This is a text ______ tells you how to use something. ______

b) Write these words next to the sentences in a).

| doctor • flag • instruction • sheep • Welsh |
|---|

## Extra practice 8

▸ page 117

a) Look at the German words. Write the English words.

1 eine Vloggerin ______

2 ein Tool ______

3 ein Filter ______

**Tipp:** Nomen werden im Englischen meist kleingeschrieben.

b) Now match[4] these words. Draw lines[5].

| | |
|---|---|
| 1 deleted | A *Drache* |
| 2 important | B *gelöscht* |
| 3 dragon | C *wichtig* |

c) Complete the sentences with the correct English words from a) and b).

1 The *vlogger* was unhappy with her video, so she ______ it.

2 A ______ is a ______ that you can use to make your photo look better.

3 The ______ is on the Welsh flag. It's an ______ symbol in Wales.

[1] **complete** *ergänzen* [2] **sentence** *Satz* [3] **symbol** *Symbol* [4] **match** *zuordnen* [5] **line** *Linie*

## Unit 4
## Wales: Digital life

| | | |
|---|---|---|
| ▸ p. 102 | **donkey** | der Esel |
| | **energy** | die Energie |
| | **national** | national |
| | **sheep**, *pl* **sheep** | das Schaf |

a **donkey**

! one **sheep** – two **sheep**

| | | |
|---|---|---|
| ▸ p. 103 | **Welsh** | walisisch, das Walisisch (Sprache) |
| | **million** | Million |
| | **social media** *(pl)* | die sozialen Medien |

## Topic 1

| | | |
|---|---|---|
| ▸ p. 104 | (to) **finish** | enden; beenden, zu Ende machen |
| | **mine** | meine, meiner, meins |

! **Possessive pronouns**

| | | |
|---|---|---|
| I | ▸ mine | meine, meiner, meins |
| you | ▸ yours | deine, deiner, deins; Ihrer, Ihre, Ihres |
| he | ▸ his | seiner, seine, seins |
| she | ▸ hers | ihrer, ihre, ihres |
| it | ▸ its | seiner, seine, seins; ihrer, ihre, ihrs |
| we | ▸ ours | unserer, unsere, unseres |
| you | ▸ yours | eurer, eure, eures; Ihrer, Ihre, Ihres |
| they | ▸ theirs | ihrer, ihre, ihrs |

| | | |
|---|---|---|
| | (to) **choose: I chose** | ich habe gewählt |

## Topic 2

| | | |
|---|---|---|
| ▸ p. 107 | **medicine** *(no pl)* | die Medizin; das Medikament, die Medikamente |
| | **mother** | die Mutter |

a **mother**

| | | |
|---|---|---|
| | (to) **see a doctor** | einen Arzt / eine Ärztin aufsuchen |
| | **doctor** | der Arzt, die Ärztin |
| | **yesterday** | gestern |
| | **father** | der Vater |

a **father**

| | | |
|---|---|---|
| ▸ p. 108 | **instruction** | die Anweisung; die Anleitung |
| | (to) **charge (a phone/ smartwatch/...)** | aufladen *(Telefon, Smartwatch usw.)* |
| | (to) **tap sth.** | tippen *an/auf etwas* |
| | (to) **download** | herunterladen |
| | (to) **switch sth. on/off** | etwas einschalten / ausschalten |

| | | |
|---|---|---|
| ▸ p. 109 | (to) **explain** | erklären |
| | **setting** | das Setting *(die Einstellung, z. B. bei Geräten)* |
| | **language** | die Sprache |

## Topic 3

| | | |
|---|---|---|
| ▸ p. 110 | (to) **delete** | löschen |
| | **feeling** | das Gefühl |
| ▸ p. 111 | **profile** | das Profil; die Beschreibung, das Portrait |
| | (to) **upload** | uploaden, hochladen |
| | **private** | privat; persönlich |
| | **public** | öffentlich |
| | **biography** (*kurz auch:* **bio**) | die Biografie |
| | **a few** | einige |
| ▸ p. 112 | **fact** | die Tatsache |
| | **cyberbullying** | das Cybermobbing |
| | (to) **research** | erforschen, untersuchen, recherchieren |
| | **people that work for ...** | Leute, die für ... arbeiten |
| | (to) **experience sth.** | etwas erfahren; erleben |

| | | |
|---|---|---|
| | (to) **bully** | mobben |
| | **news** | die Nachricht(en) |
| | **a teenager who / teenagers who** | ein Teenager, der ... / Teenager, die ... |
| | **victim** | das Opfer |
| | **terrible** | schrecklich, fürchterlich |
| | **daughter** | die Tochter |

| | | |
|---|---|---|
| ▸ p. 113 | (to) **subscribe to sth.** | etwas abonnieren |

## Story

| | | |
|---|---|---|
| ▸ p. 114 | (to) **edit** | bearbeiten, editieren |
| | (to) **get annoyed** | sich ärgern |
| | **exchange** | der Schüleraustausch |
| | **the next day** | am nächsten Tag |
| | (to) **post** | posten *(im Internet veröffentlichen)* |
| ▸ p. 115 | **finally** | schließlich, endlich |
| | **I guess** | ich glaube, ich nehme an |
| ▸ p. 116 | **Which influencer** do you know? | Welchen Influencer kennst du? Welche Influencerin kennst du? |
| | **filter** | der Filter |
| | **lighting** | die Beleuchtung |
| | **pose** | die Pose, die Haltung |

## Study skills

| | | |
|---|---|---|
| ▸ p. 118 | **habit** | die (An-)Gewohnheit |

**Irregular verbs**

| **Infinitive** | **Simple past** | **Past participle** | |
|---|---|---|---|
| (to) **choose** | **chose** | **chosen** | (aus)wählen |
| (to) **drive** | **drove** | **driven** | (mit dem Auto) fahren |
| (to) **meet** | **met** | **met** | treffen |
| (to) **sit** | **sat** | **sat** | sitzen, sich setzen |
| (to) **write** | **wrote** | **written** | schreiben |

# Unit 5
# Two Irelands: Together

A The Titanic Belfast museum

B The Giant's Causeway

C Belfast's Peace Walls

## 1 Listening **North & South Together**

a) Before you listen **The *North & South Together* project wants to keep peace[1] in Northern Ireland and Ireland. Jack and Orla are members of this project. Look at the photos of Jack and Orla above and read the speech bubbles[2].**

Who is from Ireland? ___________ Who is from Northern Ireland? ___________

b) **Look at the photos on** pages 130–131 **and read the captions[3]. Then listen to Jack and Orla and put the photos in the right order. Write 1–6.**

[1] **keep peace** *Frieden erhalten* [2] **speech bubble** *Sprechblase* [3] **caption** *Bildunterschrift*

## Nach dieser Unit kann ich ...

- ○ über Irland und Nordirland sprechen
- ○ eine Reise planen und darüber reden

F

Live music in Dublin ☐

D

King John's Castle in Limerick ☐

E

Dublin's St Patrick's Day Parade ☐

**c) Listen again. Are the sentences[1] true (✓) or false[2] (✗)?**

1 Jack thinks that peace is important. ☐
2 His parents weren't scared. ☐
3 He likes the Titanic Belfast museum. ☐
4 Orla has been to Northern Ireland before. ☐
5 King John's Castle is over 800 years old. ☐
6 The best St Patrick's Day Parade is in Limerick. ☐

**d) Look at photos 1–6 again. What would you like to see or do? Tell each other.**

*I want to see / go to / listen to ...*

▸ Extra practice 1, p. 136

[1] sentence *Satz* [2] false *falsch*

Digital quiz — Ich kann über Irland und Nordirland sprechen. ✓

# In Belfast

## 1 Reading **Sights in Belfast**

a) Before you read **Write the names in the box[1] over the correct[2] sight.**

| |
|---|
| Belfast Castle • St George's Market • The Murals • The Titanic Belfast museum |

www.example.com/belfast-sights

A

You have to see Belfast's amazing street art! They show Belfast's history as well as things that are happening today.

B

Do you want to have the best view of Belfast? Go to this famous old building. You can also take a break in the beautiful green park.

C

Are you hungry? From Friday to Sunday you can enjoy the food, shop for special gifts and listen to local musicians.

D

Have you heard of the *Titanic*? Sadly, this famous ship never finished its journey. It was made in Belfast, so it is an important part of our history here.

b) **Scan the website. Where can you do these things? Write letters A–D.**

1 enjoy a park ☐

2 learn about a sad journey ☐

3 go shopping ☐

4 learn about Belfast's history ☐ ☐

Das *Scanning* hilft dir, bestimmte Informationen zu finden, ohne jedes Wort lesen zu müssen. Überlege dir Schlüsselwörter, überfliege den Text und suche nach diesen Schlüsselwörtern.

[1] **box** *Kasten* [2] **correct** *richtig*

## 2 Speaking **Staying in Belfast**

a) Partner B: Look at page 136.
Partner A: Read about *The Beyond B&B* and answer the questions.
Write the answers in the table.

| | Beyond B&B | Ivy House |
|---|---|---|
| How much is it? | ______ | £85 / £95 |
| Does the room have its own bathroom? | ______ | yes / no |
| Is there a hot breakfast? | ______ | yes / no |

**The Beyond B&B**

The *Beyond B&B* is in the centre of Belfast. Our comfortable rooms (£85) share a bathroom with two other rooms. Each room also has a TV and a kettle.

Every morning we have a hot breakfast of eggs, sausages and tomatoes. We have vegetarian food as well.

b) Ask partner B the three questions about *Ivy House*. Circle[1] the right answers in the table.

c) Where would you like to stay? Why?

## 3 Listening **At the competition**

a) Before you listen **Do you like to dance?**

b) **Listen and circle the right answer.**

1 At the start, Orla is nervous about A Declan B Jack C her dance.
2 She arrived in Belfast A yesterday B two days ago C three days ago.
3 Declan is from A Ireland B Limerick C Belfast.
4 At the end, Orla is nervous about A Declan B Jack C her dance.

c) **What do you think will happen next? Write three sentences[2].**

be mean to ... • be the winner of the competition • see ... again • have a great day tomorrow • ...

I think Orla will ______________________________.

Maybe Jack will ______________________________.

I think Declan won't ______________________________.

[1] **circle** *umkreisen* [2] **sentence** *Satz*

Digital quiz Ich kann **eine Reise planen und darüber reden.**

# Tina times two

## 1 A wish

Before you watch **In the video Tina makes a wish. What would you wish for?**

I would wish for ______________________________.

a new bike • a games console • a pet • cool shoes • a trip to my grandparents • ...

## 2 Viewing 'I'm Tina too'

**Watch the first part of the video. Are the sentences[1] true (✓) or false[2] (✗)?**

1 Tina doesn't like dancing. ☐

2 Tina's parents don't listen to her. ☐

3 Tina's parents forget her birthday. ☐

4 Tina 2 is more confident than Tina. ☐

## 3 Viewing 'I had the most absolutely amazing day today'

a) **What do you think Tina 2 is going to do?**

go to the dance class • speak to Tina's parents • dance in the street • do something mean • ...

I think Tina 2 is going to ______________________________.

b) **Watch the second[3] part of the video and check.**

## 4 'Don't be scared – be spectacular!'

**How does Tina feel? Draw lines[4].**

| | |
|---|---|
| 1 When she first meets the boy: | confident |
| 2 When Tina 2 puts her in the wardrobe: | scared |
| 3 When she dances with her class at the end: | angry |

[1] **sentence** *Satz* [2] **false** *falsch* [3] **second** *zweite(r,s)* [4] **line** *Linie*

## 1 Reading Two countries

Ich kann über Irland und Nordirland sprechen.

**Scan this text and answer the questions.**

www.example.com/twoirelands

### Ireland and Northern Ireland

- People speak Irish and English in both[1] countries. More people speak Irish in Ireland than in Northern Ireland.
- Northern Ireland is part of the UK, but it isn't in the EU. Ireland isn't part of the UK, but it is in the EU.
- Both countries have a capital city. Dublin is the capital city of Ireland and Belfast is the capital city of Northern Ireland.
- Money is different in both countries. If you want to buy something in Ireland, you pay in Euros. In Northern Ireland you pay with pounds, like in England.

1 What languages do people speak in both countries? ______

2 Which country is part of the UK? ______

3 What are the capital cities? ______

4 What kind of money do you need? ______

## 2 Listening Phoning a hotel

Ich kann eine Reise planen und darüber reden.

**a) Joe phones a hotel. Listen and put the pictures in the right order. Write 1–5.**

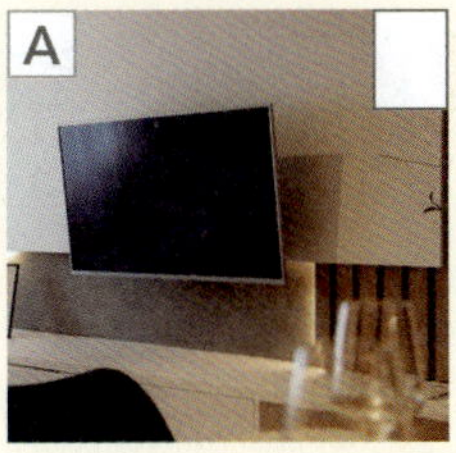

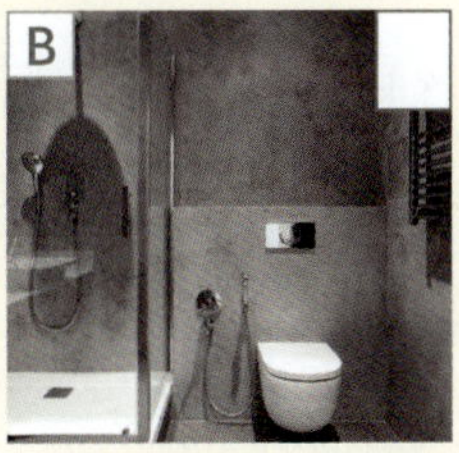

**b) Listen again. Are the sentences true (✓) or false (✗)?**

1 Joe wants a room for tomorrow. ☐

2 The hotel has a room free. ☐

3 The room Joe wants costs 65 euros. ☐

4 Breakfast is in the price. ☐

5 The room has a kettle. ☐

6 They will get to the hotel in the evening. ☐

Check

1 both *beide*

# Partner page

## 2 Speaking Staying in Belfast ▸ page 133

a) Partner B: Read about *Ivy House B&B* and answer the questions. Write the answers in the table.

| | Ivy House | Beyond B&B |
|---|---|---|
| How much is it? | ______ | £85 / £95 |
| Does the room have its own bathroom? | ______ | yes / no |
| Is there a hot breakfast? | ______ | yes / no |

Our large rooms have their own bathroom with a shower. There are free bottles of water in every room as well as a kettle. Rooms are £95 with breakfast.

Guests can use our free internet and relax in the garden. Enjoy a great breakfast of muesli, fruit, yoghurt, cheese, cold meat[1] and bread.

b) Now ask partner B the three questions about *The Beyond B&B*. Choose the right answers in the table.

c) Where would you like to stay? Why?

# Extra practice

### Extra practice 1 ▸ page 131

Match the definitions[2] to the words.

| | |
|---|---|
| 1 A big, old building with walls, often where a king lived a long time ago. | a peace |
| 2 Very big and strong monsters from old legends | b giants |
| 3 When people celebrate outside and walk together, often with music. | c Peace Walls |
| 4 Walls in Northern Ireland that keep people from each other. | d murals |
| 5 Pictures that people draw on walls. | e parade |
| 6 When there is no fighting. | f castle |

[1] **cold meat** *Aufschnitt* [2] **definition** *Erklärung*

## °Unit 5
## Northern Ireland: Together

Die Unit 5 ist keine Pflicht-Unit, daher sind die neuen Wörter mit einem Kringel (°) markiert. Wenn ihr die Unit bearbeitet, kannst du die neuen Wörter lernen, aber sie werden in Band 4 nicht vorausgesetzt.

| | | |
|---|---|---|
| ▸ p. 130 | **°giant** | der Riese, die Riesin |
| | **°peace** | der Friede(n) |

### In Belfast

| | | |
|---|---|---|
| ▸ p. 132 | **°mural** | das Wandgemälde |
| | **°view (of)** | die Aussicht (auf) |
| | **°local** | einheimisch, am/vom Ort |
| | **°ship** | das Schiff |
| | °(to) **scan (a text)** | (einen Text) überfliegen |
| ▸ p. 133 | **°B&B (bed and breakfast)** | die Frühstückspension |
| | °(to) **share sth.** | sich etw. teilen |
| | **°each** | jede(r, s) (einzelne), jeweils |
| | **°kettle** | der Wasserkocher *(elektrisch)* |
| | **°vegetarian** | vegetarisch |
| | **°large** | groß |
| | **°guest** | der Gast |
| | **°muesli** | das Müsli |
| | **°nervous** | nervös, aufgeregt |

a **ship**

a **kettle**

**muesli**

### Viewing

| | | |
|---|---|---|
| ▸ p. 134 | **°times** | mal |
| | **°wish** | der Wunsch |
| | °(to) **wish (for sth.)** | (sich etwas) wünschen |
| | **°absolutely** | total, absolut, vollkommen |
| | **°spectacular** | spektakulär, aufsehenerregend |

| infinitive | simple past | past participle | |
|---|---|---|---|
| (to) **be** | **was/were** | **been** | *sein* |
| (to) **become** | **became** | **become** | *werden* |
| (to) **blow** | **blew** | **blown** | *blasen, pusten* |
| (to) **bring** | **brought** | **brought** | *(mit)bringen* |
| (to) **buy** | **bought** | **bought** | *kaufen* |
| (to) **choose** | **chose** | **chosen** | *(aus)wählen* |
| (to) **come** | **came** | **come** | *kommen* |
| (to) **cost** | **cost** | **cost** | *kosten* |
| (to) **cut** | **cut** | **cut** | *schneiden* |
| (to) **do** | **did** | **done** | *tun* |
| (to) **draw** | **drew** | **drawn** | *zeichnen* |
| (to) **drink** | **drank** | **drunk** | *trinken* |
| (to) **drive** | **drove** | **driven** | *(mit dem Auto) fahren* |
| (to) **eat** | **ate** | **eaten** | *essen* |
| (to) **fall** | **fell** | **fallen** | *fallen* |
| (to) **feel** | **felt** | **felt** | *(sich) fühlen* |
| (to) **fight** | **fought** | **fought** | *kämpfen* |
| (to) **find** | **found** | **found** | *finden* |
| (to) **fly** | **flew** | **flown** | *fliegen* |
| (to) **forget** | **forgot** | **forgotten** | *vergessen* |
| (to) **get** | **got** | **got** | *bekommen, werden* |
| (to) **give** | **gave** | **given** | *geben* |
| (to) **go** | **went** | **gone** | *gehen* |
| (to) **have** | **had** | **had** | *haben* |
| (to) **hear** | **heard** | **heard** | *hören* |
| (to) **hurt** | **hurt** | **hurt** | *schmerzen, wehtun* |
| (to) **keep** | **kept** | **kept** | *halten, behalten* |
| (to) **know** | **knew** | **known** | *wissen; kennen* |
| (to) **leave** | **left** | **left** | *verlassen* |
| (to) **let** | **let** | **let** | *lassen* |
| (to) **lose** | **lost** | **lost** | *verlieren* |
| (to) **make** | **made** | **made** | *machen* |

| infinitive | simple past | past participle | |
|---|---|---|---|
| (to) **meet** | **met** | **met** | *treffen* |
| (to) **pay** | **paid** | **paid** | *bezahlen* |
| (to) **put** | **put** | **put** | *legen, stellen* |
| (to) **read** | **read** | **read** | *lesen* |
| (to) **ride** | **rode** | **ridden** | *reiten; (Rad) fahren* |
| (to) **run** | **ran** | **run** | *rennen* |
| (to) **say** | **said** | **said** | *sagen* |
| (to) **see** | **saw** | **seen** | *sehen* |
| (to) **sell** | **sold** | **sold** | *verkaufen* |
| (to) **send** | **sent** | **sent** | *senden, schicken* |
| (to) **set the table** | **set** | **set** | *den Tisch decken* |
| (to) **show** | **showed** | **shown** | *zeigen* |
| (to) **sing** | **sang** | **sung** | *singen* |
| (to) **sit** | **sat** | **sat** | *sitzen, sich setzen* |
| (to) **sleep** | **slept** | **slept** | *schlafen* |
| (to) **speak** | **spoke** | **spoken** | *sprechen* |
| (to) **spend** | **spent** | **spent** | *(Geld) ausgeben, (Zeit) verbringen* |
| (to) **swim** | **swam** | **swum** | *schwimmen* |
| (to) **take** | **took** | **taken** | *nehmen; (Zeit) dauern* |
| (to) **tell** | **told** | **told** | *erzählen* |
| (to) **think** | **thought** | **thought** | *denken* |
| (to) **understand** | **understood** | **understood** | *verstehen* |
| (to) **wear** | **wore** | **worn** | *tragen, anhanben* |
| (to) **win** | **won** | **won** | *gewinnen, siegen* |
| (to) **write** | **wrote** | **written** | *schreiben* |

## Wordbank 1: On the street

▸ Unit 1 | p. 21

*Excuse me, how do I get to …? /*
*Sorry, I'm lost. Could you tell me the way to …?*

### Directions

Go straight on.

Turn left.

Turn right.

Take the first / second / third street on the left / right.

Go across the road.

Go along the river.

Go down the steps.

Go over the bridge.

Go past the cinema.

Go to the end of the street.

Go through the park.

Go up the hill.

### Places

block of flats

car park

office building

petrol station

roundabout

skyscraper

traffic lights

zebra crossing

## Wordbank 2: Giving opinions

▸ Unit 1 | p. 25

| Words for 'good' |
| --- |
| amazing |
| awesome |
| brilliant |
| cool |
| excellent |
| fantastic |
| fine |
| great |
| perfect |
| wonderful |

| Words for 'bad' |
| --- |
| awful |
| horrible |
| lousy |
| nasty |
| not my thing |
| poor |
| rubbish |
| shocking |
| terrible |
| useless |

## Wordbank 3: Describing clothes and accessories

▸ Unit 2 | p. 46, 47

**Materials** *(Materialien)*

canvas *(Segeltuch)*

cotton *(Baumwolle)*

leather *(Leder)*

metal *(Metall)*

polyester *(Polyester)*

rubber *(Gummi)*

silk *(Seide)*

wool *(Wolle)*

**Colours and patterns** *(Farben und Muster)*

checked *(kariert)*

colourful *(farbenfroh)*

dark / light *(dunkel / hell)*

flowery *(geblümt)*

patterned *(gemustert)*

plain *(einfarbig)*

dotted *(gepunktet)*

striped *(gestreift)*

**fit (Passform)**
- baggy
- tight

**style**
- cool
- casual
- trendy
- unusual
- designer
- sporty
- vintage
- smart

**(to) buy clothes**
- shop
- shopping centre
- online
- **"green"**
  - second-hand
  - recycled
  - eco-friendly
  - flea-market

## Wordbank 4: Feelings

▶ Unit 2 | p. 54
▶ Unit 4 | p. 105

| | |
|---|---|
| all right / OK | *in Ordnung* |
| amazing | *fantastisch, erstaunlich* |
| brave | *mutig* |
| calm | *ruhig, besonnen* |
| cheerful | *fröhlich* |
| confident | *selbstbewusst, sicher* |
| content | *zufrieden* |
| creative | *kreativ* |
| energetic | *energiegeladen, aktiv* |
| excellent | *hervorragend* |
| excited | *aufgeregt, gespannt* |
| fantastic | *fantastisch* |
| fine | *gut, prima* |
| great | *großartig* |
| happy | *froh, glücklich* |
| motivated | *motiviert* |
| proud | *stolz* |
| relaxed | *entspannt* |
| strong | *stark* |
| surprised | *überrascht* |
| wonderful | *wunderbar* |

| | |
|---|---|
| angry | *wütend, zornig* |
| awful | *schrecklich* |
| bored | *gelangweilt* |
| disappointed | *enttäuscht* |
| embarrassed | *peinlich berührt, verlegen* |
| fed up | *genervt, sauer* |
| frustrated | *frustiert* |
| horrible | *schrecklich* |
| jealous | *eifersüchtig* |
| lonely | *einsam* |
| nasty | *scheußlich* |
| nervous | *nervös* |
| puzzled | *verwirrt, ratlos* |
| sad | *traurig* |
| scared | *verängstigt* |
| shocked | *schockiert* |
| stressed | *gestresst* |
| terrible | *furchtbar* |
| tired | *müde* |
| upset | *aufgeregt, bestürzt* |
| useless | *nutzlos* |
| worried | *besorgt* |

## Wordbank 5: Scary creatures

▶ Unit 3 | p. 76, 77

**I know a scary story about a / an ...**
dragon, ghost, mermaid, merman, monster, vampire

demon

gargoyle

goblin

mummy

ogre

werewolf

witch

wizard

zombie

## Wordbank 6: Sports

▶ Unit 2 | p. 56
▶ Unit 3 | p. 81

**I play ...**

badminton, basketball, cricket, football, hockey, table tennis, tennis

handball

rugby

volleyball

**I go ...**

bowling, climbing, cycling, dancing, hiking, horse riding, paddleboarding, running, skateboarding, skiing, surfing, swimming, walking

canoeing

ice skating

rowing

**I do ...**

fitness, karate, trampolining, yoga

archery

athletics

boxing

scuba diving

gymnastics

judo

## Wordbank 7: Nature

▶ Unit 3 | p. 82, 83

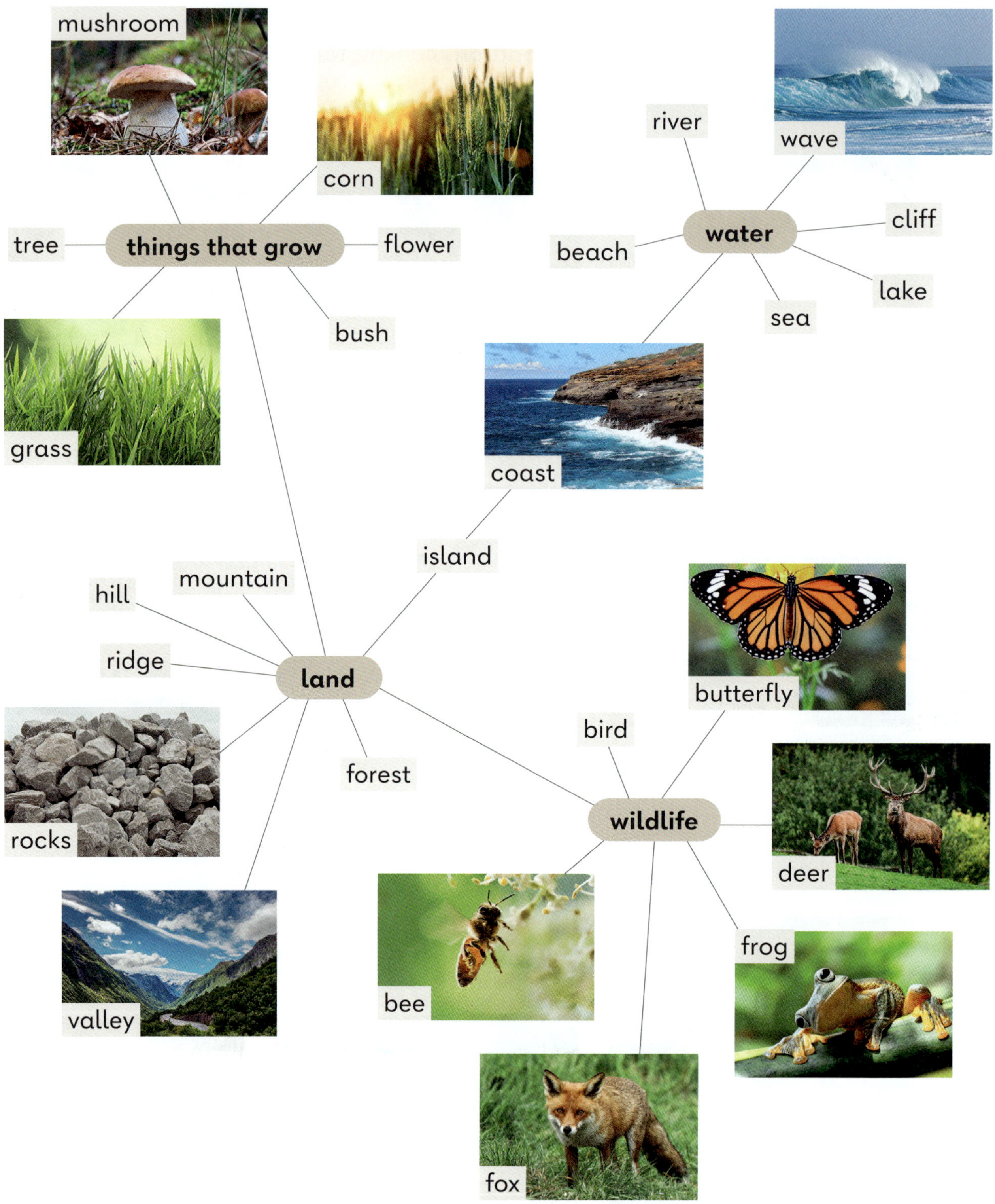


| | |
|---|---|
| a beautiful / wild landscape | *eine schöne / wilde Landschaft* |
| a blue / cloudy sky | *ein blauer / bewölkter Himmel* |
| a narrow / wide river | *ein schmaler / breiter Fluss* |
| a high mountain | *ein hoher Berg* |
| a sandy / rocky beach | *ein Sandstrand / ein steiniger Strand* |

## Wordbank 8: Sights and places to visit

▸ Unit 4 | p. 103

**In my area there is a/an …**

art gallery, castle, escape room, library, museum, TV tower, theatre, zoo

harbour

national park

old town

palace

theme park

tower

town hall

town / village square

waterfall

## Wordbank 9: Tech instructions

▶ Unit 4 | p. 108

**Show the order of instructions**

First ... / Second ... / Third ...
Then ... / Next ... / After that ...
Finally...

**Get started**

(to) switch on / off a device
(to) charge a device / a laptop / a tablet
(to) check the connection
(to) connect to Wi-Fi
(to) enter / put in a password
(to) log on

**Prepare**

(to) choose / download an app / software / a program
(to) install an app / software / a program
(to) pair with another device
(to) set up a device

**Use a device**

(to) click on a link (with a mouse)
(to) press a key (on a keyboard)
(to) scroll up / down a page
(to) swipe a screen
(to) tap an icon
(to) use a search engine

**Files, texts and videos**

(to) add captions / music / text effects
(to) copy / cut / paste text
(to) edit a text / video / vlog
(to) save data / a file
(to) upload a file / photos / a video

**Cover**

Cornelsen/li.: Shutterstock.com/Ron Ellis/courtesy of Transport for London; Personen: Chocolate Films; Hintergrund re.: stock.adobe.com/anatoliycherkas; U3: Cornelsen/Carlos Borrell Eiköter

**Illustrationen**

Cornelsen/Carlos Borrell Eiköter: S. 26; Cornelsen/Harald Ardeias: S. 6, S. 7, S. 21, S. 22, S. 23, S. 32, S. 52, S. 55, S. 56, S. 57, S. 62, S. 65, S. 67, S. 77, S. 82, S. 84, S. 85, S. 86, S. 90, S. 123, S. 140; Cornelsen/Inhouse/Josephine Bienert-Köhler: S. 93, S. 144; Cornelsen/Inhouse/Melina Frick: S. 34/l.; Cornelsen/Jeongsook Lee: S. 127/m.; Shutterstock.com/Artisticco: S. 40/C; Ungermeyer: S. 34/United, S. 92/United

**Fotos**

S. 2: PEFC Deutschland e.V.; S. 3: Cornelsen/Inhouse/Anne Weingarten; S. 4/Flaggen: Shutterstock.com/SLdesign; S. 4/Karte: Shutterstock.com/Peter Hermes Furian; S. 4/Mädchen: Cornelsen/Chocolate Films; S. 4/Mann: Shutterstock.com/Dieter Hawlan; S. 4/u.: stock.adobe.com/Tomas Marek; S. 5/1 v.o.n.u.: stock.adobe.com/sborisov; S. 5/2: mauritius images/age fotostock; S. 5/3: stock.adobe.com/Юлия Клюева; S. 5/4: Shutterstock.com/Tyler Olson; S. 5/5: mauritius images/Steve Vidler; S. 5/6: Digital Learning Ass. Ltd.; S. 5/7: Shutterstock.com/Eszter Szadeczky-Kardoss; S. 5/8: mauritius images/alamy stock photo/Jeffrey Isaac Greenberg 3+; S. 6/1 v.o.n.u.: Cornelsen/Chocolate Films; S. 6/2: Shutterstock.com/insta_photos; S. 6/3: Shutterstock.com/LightField Studios; S. 6/4: Interfilm Berlin Management; S. 6/5: Shutterstock.com/Marian Fil; S. 6/6: Shutterstock.com/BearFotos; S. 7/1 v.o.n.u.: stock.adobe.com/moofushi; S. 7/2: Imago Stock & People GmbH/imagebroker/RolandxMarske; S. 7/3: stock.adobe.com/Duncan Andison; S. 7/4: Digital Learning Ass. Ltd.; S. 7/5: Shutterstock.com/Lubomira08; S. 8/1 v.o.n.u.: stock.adobe.com/Huebi; S. 8/2: stock.adobe.com/Richard Whitcombe; S. 8/3: mauritius images/Westend61; S. 8/4: Shutterstock.com/stockfour; S. 8/5: Cornelsen/Person re.: Chocolate Films, Wagen + Hintergrund: mauritius images/PHILIP SMITH/Alamy; S. 8/6: Digital Learning Ass. Ltd.; S. 8/7: stock.adobe.com/Krakenimages.com; S. 8/8: stock.adobe.com/Good Studio; S. 9/m.: stock.adobe.com/BCFC; S. 9/o.: mauritius images/Hemis.fr; S. 9/u.: Interfilm Berlin Management; S. 10/Flaggen: Shutterstock.com/SLdesign; S. 10/Karte: Shutterstock.com/Peter Hermes Furian; S. 11: Cornelsen/Chocolate Films; S. 12/A: mauritius images/Alexander Pöschel; S. 12/B: Shutterstock.com/Dieter Hawlan; S. 12/C: stock.adobe.com/zgphotography; S. 12/u.: Cornelsen/Chocolate Films; S. 13/D: mauritius images/Prisma; S. 13/E: stock.adobe.com/Tomas Marek; S. 13/F: stock.adobe.com/coward_lion; S. 14/A: mauritius images/Novarc Images; S. 14/B: stock.adobe.com/sborisov; S. 14/Junge: Cornelsen/Chocolate Films; S. 14/Mädchen: Cornelsen/Anja Poehlmann; S. 15/C: Imago Stock & People GmbH/Westend61; S. 15/D: stock.adobe.com/Mistervlad; S. 15/E: stock.adobe.com/Photocreo Bednarek; S. 16/m.: Shutterstock.com/Sampajano_Anizza; S. 16/o.: mauritius images/age fotostock; S. 16/u.: mauritius images/Simon Belcher; S. 17: stock.adobe.com/I-Wei Huang; S. 18/A: Imago Stock&People GmbH/Jeff Greenberg; S. 18/B: mauritius images/alamy stock photo/Scott Sim; S. 18/C: stock.adobe.com/Юлия Клюева; S. 19: Cornelsen/Chocolate Films; S. 20: stock.adobe.com/Nicola; S. 22/1 l.v.o.n.u.: Shutterstock.com/Pixel-Shot; S. 22/2: Shutterstock.com/MariaKovaleva; S. 22/3: Shutterstock.com/diplomedia; S. 22/4: Shutterstock.com/Veliavik; S. 22/5: Shutterstock.com/diplomedia; S. 22/6: Shutterstock.com/OlgaBombologna; S. 22/u.r.: stock.adobe.com/anaumenko; S. 23: Shutterstock.com/fizkes; S. 24/o.: Shutterstock.com/Tyler Olson; S. 24/u.: stock.adobe.com/FotoStuss; S. 25: SDG wheel: courtesy of the UNITED NATIONS/Department of Global Communications (https:// www.un.org/sustainabledevelopment)/The content of this publication has not been approved by the United Nations and does not reflect the views of the United Nations or its officials or Member States.); S. 26/m.r.: stock.adobe.com/Richie Chan; S. 26/u.r.: mauritius images/Steve Vidler; S. 27/m.: Cornelsen/Personen: Chocolate Films, Hintergrund: mauritius images/alamy stock photo/Fotomaton; S. 27/o.: mauritius images/Loop Images; S. 27/u.: mauritius images/Steve Vidler; S. 29: Digital Learning Ass. Ltd.; S. 30/A: Shutterstock.com/TTstudio; S. 30/B: Shutterstock.com/Eszter Szadeczky-Kardoss; S. 31/o.: mauritius images/alamy stock photo/Jeffrey Isaac Greenberg 3+; S. 31/u.: mauritius images/Westend61; S. 32: stock.adobe.com/pxl.store; S. 33/m.: Shutterstock.com/Damir Khabirov; S. 33/o.l.: Shutterstock.com/Vector FX; S. 33/o.r.: Shutterstock/Dyek Marina; S. 33/u.: Shutterstock.com/paulaphoto; S. 34/Flagge: Shutterstock.com/SLdesign; S. 34/r.: Cornelsen/ Chocolate Films; S. 35/m.l.: Shutterstock.com/I Wei Huang; S. 35/m.r.: mauritius images/Vantage; S. 35/o.: Shutterstock.com/Monkey Business Images; S. 35/u.: mauritius images/alamy stock photo/ Alex Segre; S. 37: Shutterstock.com/Mizanur Rahman razu; S. 39/A: Imago Stock&People GmbH/ Loop Images/Peter Noyce/LOOP IMAGES PNE991430\r\n\r; S. 39/B: stock.adobe.com/Jaroslav Moravcik; S. 39/C: stock.adobe.com/Denis Feldmann; S. 39/D: stock.adobe.com/I-Wei Huang; S. 39/E: Shutterstock.com/andersphoto; S. 39/F: Shutterstock.com/alice-photo; S. 40/A: Shutterstock.com/RedlineVector; S. 40/B: Shutterstock.com/Boule; S. 40/D: Shutterstock.com/ClassicVector; S. 40/E: Shutterstock.com/PavKon; S. 41/m.: stock.adobe.com/EMrpize; S. 41/o.: stock.adobe.com/mipan; S. 41/u.: stock.adobe.com/Elenarts; S. 42/2.v.o.: stock.adobe.com/Diana Taliun; S. 42/3.v.o.: stock.adobe.com/sommai; S. 42/o.: Shutterstock.com/Rvector; S. 42/u.: Shutterstock.com/worradirek; S. 43/o.: stock.adobe.com/New Africa; S. 43/u.: Shutterstock.com/Patra.K; S. 44/ Emoji: Shutterstock.com/Magnos Weber; S. 44/m.l.: Shutterstock/Monkey Business Images; S. 44/r.: stock.adobe.com/Nicola; S. 44/Rosie: Cornelsen/Chocolate Films; S. 45/Emoji: Shutterstock.com/ Magnos Weber; S. 45/l.: Cornelsen/Chocolate Films; S. 45/m.l.: stock.adobe.com/Kaspars; S. 45/m.r.: Shutterstock.com/Spotmatik Ltd; S. 45/r.: Cornelsen/Chocolate Films; S. 46/A: Shutterstock.com/Andrey Arkusha; S. 46/B: Shutterstock.com/Kite_rin; S. 46/C: Shutterstock.com/Cast Of Thousands; S. 46/D: Shutterstock.com/insta_photos; S. 47: Shutterstock.com/Pixel-Shot; S. 48: stock.adobe.com/kleberpicui; S. 48/Emoji: Shutterstock.com/Magnos Weber; S. 49: stock.adobe.com/Jamie Grill/Blend Images; S. 50: Cornelsen/Chocolate Films; S. 51: Shutterstock.com/Light-Field Studios; S. 51/Emoji: Shutterstock.com/Magnos Weber; S. 52: Shutterstock.com/sitthiphong; S. 53: Shutterstock.com/Ververidis Vasilis; S. 54/o.: mauritius images/alamy stock photo/Jeffrey Mayer; S. 54/u.: Digital Learning Ass. Ltd.; S. 55: Shutterstock.com/sitthiphong; S. 56/A: Shutterstock.com/VectorSun58; S. 56/B: Shutterstock.com/Great_Kit; S. 56/C: Shutterstock.com/Illizium; S. 56/D: Shutterstock.com/popicon; S. 56/E: Shutterstock.com/my_design; S. 56/F: Shutterstock.com/Hasebalcon; S. 56/G: Shutterstock/Makkuro GL; S. 56/H: Shutterstock.com/Great_Kit; S. 56/I: Shutterstock.com; S. 56/u.r.: Shutterstock.com/Alexsey t17; S. 57/Emoji: Shutterstock.com/Magnos Weber; S. 57/m.l.: Shutterstock.com/Alexsey t17; S. 57/Pokal: Shutterstock.com/JosepPerianes; S. 57/u.l.: Cornelsen/Chocolate Films; S. 59: Interfilm Berlin Management; S. 60/m.l.: Shutterstock.com/Max Topchii; S. 60/o.l.: Shutterstock.com/Marian Fil; S. 60/r.: Shutterstock.com/Khosro; S. 61: Shutterstock.com/BearFotos; S. 62/1+2+4+6: Shutterstock.com/Denis Cristo; S. 62/3+5: Shutterstock.com/Lemberg Vector studio; S. 63: Shutterstock.com/tommaso79; S. 63/Emoji: Shutterstock.com/Magnos Weber; S. 64/A: mauritius images/alamy stock photo/Matthew Wilkinson; S. 64/B: mauritius images/alamy stock photo/CBW; S. 64/C: stock.adobe.com/David Matthew Lyons; S. 64/D: mauritius images/robertharding; S. 66: stock.adobe.com/Micah C/peopleimages.com; S. 68/A: stock.adobe.com/Drazen; S. 68/B: stock.adobe.com/anekoho; S. 68/C: stock.adobe.com/. shock; S. 68/D: stock.adobe.com/Ljupco Smokovski; S. 68/Döner: stock.adobe.com/Markus Mainka; S. 68/E: stock.adobe.com/Zubair; S. 68/F: stock.adobe.com/faalil; S. 68/m.r.: stock.adobe.com/ noravector; S. 68/Pizza: stock.adobe.com/whitestorm; S. 69/jacket: stock.adobe.com/Olga; S. 69/ skirt: stock.adobe.com/Tarzhanova; S. 69/socks: stock.adobe.com/Africa Studio; S. 69/u.: Shutterstock.com/Roman3dArt; S. 70/m.: Shutterstock.com/Yury Gulakov; S. 70/u.: Shutterstock.com/CLS Digital Arts; S. 71/m.: Shutterstock.com/Odua Images; S. 71/o.: Shutterstock.com/Olesia Bilkei; S. 72/o.l.: Cornelsen/Chocolate Films; S. 72/o.r.: stock.adobe.com/Sergii Figurnyi; S. 72/u.l.: mauritius images/alamy stock photo/Nicola Campbell; S. 72/u.r.: stock.adobe.com/moofushi; S. 73/o.l.: stock.adobe.com/Richie Chan; S. 73/o.r.: stock.adobe.com/Fun Altitude; S. 73/u.l.: stock.adobe.com/Apostolis Giontzis; S. 73/u.r.: mauritius images/Destinations; S. 74: Imago Stock & People GmbH/imagebroker/RolandxMarske; S. 75: stock.adobe.com/mauritius images/VisualEyze; S. 76: Cornelsen/Personen: Chocolate Films, Hintergrund: stock.adobe.com/avtk; S. 77/u.: stock.adobe.com/olizabet; S. 78/1: stock.adobe.com/EpicStockMedia; S. 78/2: mauritius images/alamy stock photo/Simon Price; S. 78/3: Shutterstock.com/coka; S. 78/4: Shutterstock.com/Vito Horak; S. 78/5: stock.adobe.com/Duncan Andison; S. 78/6: stock.adobe.com/Ellis Travel Photography/Matthew

Williams; S. 79/o.: Cornelsen/Chocolate Films; S. 79/u.: Cornelsen/Chocolate Films; S. 80: Shutterstock.com/BearFotos; S. 83: Shutterstock.com/STEKLO; S. 86: Cornelsen/Chocolate Films; S. 87: Digital Learning Ass. Ltd.; S. 87: Digital Learning Ass. Ltd. (DLA); S. 88: Shutterstock.com/Lubomira08; S. 90/o.l.: stock.adobe.com/davidionut; S. 90/o.r.: stock.adobe.com/lovelyday12; S. 91/m.l.: Shutterstock.com/Lukasz Z; S. 91/m.r.: stock.adobe.com/Pawel Gubernat; S. 91/o.l.: Shutterstock.com/eurobanks; S. 91/o.r.: Shutterstock.com/Vaclav Sonnek; S. 91/u.l.: stock.adobe.com/alexandrum01; S. 91/u.r.: stock.adobe.com/POPROTSKIY_ALEXEY/Alex Photo; S. 92/Flagge: Shutterstock.com/SLdesign; S. 92/o.l.: Shutterstock.com/Marti Bug Catcher; S. 92/o.r.: Cornelsen/Chocolate Films; S. 92/u.: stock.adobe.com/design/exclusive; S. 93/m.r.: Shutterstock.com/Moving Moment; S. 93/o.r.: mauritius images/Roger parkes/Alamy Stock Photos; S. 94: Shutterstock.com/Sudowoodo; S. 96: Shutterstock.com/Dusan Petkovic; S. 97/m.2.v.l.: Shutterstock.com/Beata Tabak; S. 97/m.2.v.r.: Shutterstock.com/HomeStudio; S. 97/m.l.: Shutterstock.com/Mirage_studio; S. 97/m.r.: Shutterstock.com/Mathee saengkaew; S. 97/o.: Shutterstock.com/Dim Tik; S. 97/u.2.v.l.: Shutterstock.com/Photos SS; S. 97/u.2.v.r.: Shutterstock/addinia; S. 97/u.l.: Shutterstock.com/gowithstock; S. 97/u.r.: Shutterstock.com/aperturesound; S. 98: Shutterstock.com/Volurol; S. 99/m.: Shutterstock.com/sirtravelalot; S. 99/o.: Shutterstock.com/Popartic; S. 99/u.: stock.adobe.com/Enrico Ferraresi; S. 100: stock.adobe.com/David Peperkamp; S. 101/m.: Shutterstock.com/lynx_v; S. 101/o.: Shutterstock.com/Denis Belitsky; S. 102/A: mauritius images/alamy stock photo/StockimoNews/Lancashire Images; S. 102/B: Shutterstock.com/Richard Whitcombe; S. 102/C: stock.adobe.com/wavebreak3; S. 102/D: stock.adobe.com/Sebastien; S. 102/o.r.: Cornelsen/Chocolate Films; S. 103/l.: Shutterstock.com/Peter Hermes Furian; S. 103/r.: stock.adobe.com/Huebi; S. 104/Emoji: Shutterstock.com/Yefym Turkin; S. 104/r.: StockFood GmbH/Look/Pompe, Ingolf; S. 105: stock.adobe.com/Richard Whitcombe; S. 106: Digital Learning Ass. Ltd.; S. 107: stock.adobe.com/studioshot; S. 108/A: stock.adobe.com/Etka; S. 108/B: Shutterstock.com/VIEW17; S. 108/C: Shutterstock.com/Pixelr Studios; S. 108/D: Shutterstock.com/GetThis; S. 108/m.: Cornelsen/Chocolate Films; S. 108/o.: Cornelsen/Chocolate Films; S. 109: mauritius images/Westend61; S. 110/m.: Shutterstock.com/izabel.l; S. 110/r.: Shutterstock.com/Roman3dArt; S. 111/A: stock.adobe.com/Belozersky; S. 111/B: stock.adobe.com/Sergey; S. 111/C: stock.adobe.com/4luck; S. 111/D: Shutterstock.com/Raura7; S. 111/r.: Cornelsen/Chocolate Films; S. 112: Shutterstock.com/LightField Studios; S. 113: Shutterstock.com/stockfour; S. 114: Cornelsen/Person re.: Chocolate Films, Wagen + Hintergrund: mauritius images/PHILIP SMITH/Alamy; S. 114/Dylan: Cornelsen/Chocolate Films; S. 114/Emoji: Shutterstock.com/Yefym Turkin; S. 115/Dylan, Cornelsen/Chocolate Films; S. 115/m.l.: Cornelsen/Person: Chocolate Films, Hintergrund: Shutterstock.com/muroPhotographer; S. 115/m.r.: Cornelsen/Junge: Cornelsen/Chocolate Films; Hintergrund: Shutterstock.com/muroPhotographer; S. 115/Emojis: Shutterstock.com/Yefym Turkin; S. 116/A: Shutterstock.com/daddy.icon; S. 116/B: Shutterstock.com/koblizeek; S. 116/C: Shutterstock.com/Dreamerdesign; S. 116/D: Shutterstock.com/Leremy; S. 116/E: Shutterstock.com/sore88; S. 116/F: Shutterstock.com/Rawpixel Ltd.; S. 117/m.: Digital Learning Ass. Ltd.; S. 117/o.: Shutterstock.com/gritsalak karalak; S. 118: stock.adobe.com/Krakenimages.com; S. 119: stock.adobe.com/Good Studio; S. 120/m.: Shutterstock.com/Tomas Marek; S. 120/o.: stock.adobe.com/Colin & Linda McKie; S. 120/u.: stock.adobe.com/JoeE Jackson; S. 122/o.: mauritius images/Westend61; S. 122/u.: Shutterstock.com/stockfour; S. 124/m.: stock.adobe.com/Jackie Davies; S. 124/o.: stock.adobe.com/Richard Whitcombe; S. 124/u.: stock.adobe.com/Alexey Fedorenko; S. 125/A: Shutterstock.com/lazyllama; S. 125/B: Shutterstock.com/Gorodenkoff; S. 125/C: Shutterstock.com/Roman Samborskyi; S. 125/D: Shutterstock/guteksk7; S. 125/E: Shutterstock.com/Ayesha kanwal; S. 125/F: Shutterstock.com/CHIARI VFX; S. 125/o.: stock.adobe.com/bank215; S. 126: stock.adobe.com/Huebi; S. 127/o.: Shutterstock.com/photomaster; S. 127/u.: Shutterstock.com/GoodStudio; S. 128/m.: stock.adobe.com/Matthew Gilbert; S. 128/o.: Shutterstock.com/SunshineVector; S. 129: Shutterstock.com/optiplex studio; S. 130/A: mauritius images/Hemis.fr; S. 130/B: stock.adobe.com/aitormmfoto; S. 130/C: mauritius images/SagaPhoto; S. 130/o.l.: Cornelsen/Chocolate Films; S. 130/o.r.: stock.adobe.com/Peter Hermes Furian; S. 131/D: stock.adobe.com/Eugene Remizov; S. 131/E: mauritius images/alamy stock photo/Striking Images - Tourism Ireland; S. 131/F: mauritius images/Rene Mattes; S. 131/o.r.: Cornelsen/

Chocolate Films; S. 132/A: mauritius images/Loop Images/Extramural Activity; S. 132/B: stock.adobe.com/hunterbliss; S. 132/C: mauritius images/alamy stock photo/Jane Sweeney; S. 132/D: mauritius images/John Warburton-Lee; S. 133: stock.adobe.com/BCFC; S. 134: Interfilm Berlin Management; S. 135/1 v.l.n.r.: stock.adobe.com/triocean; S. 135/2: stock.adobe.com/brizmaker; S. 135/3: Shutterstock.com/Ihor Khobta; S. 135/4: stock.adobe.com/bit24; S. 135/5: stock.adobe.com/ti_to_tito; S. 136: Shutterstock.com/Duncan Andison; S. 137/m.: Shutterstock.com/Vydrin; S. 137/o.: Shutterstock.com/Federico Rostagno; S. 137/u.: Shutterstock.com/Yulia Davidovich; S. 140/block o.f.: stock.adobe.com/bzyxx; S. 140/car park: stock.adobe.com/Zoe; S. 140/o.r.: Shutterstock.com/Barbara Sauder; S. 140/office: stock.adobe.com/william87; S. 140/petrol st.: stock.adobe.com/Carolyn Franks; S. 140/roundabout: stock.adobe.com/Sampajano-Anizza; S. 140/skyscraper: stock.adobe.com/Rich Lindie; S. 140/traffic l.: stock.adobe.com/alice_photo; S. 140/zebra c.: Shutterstock.com/Claudio Divizia; S. 141/Emoji: stock.adobe.com/jehafo; S. 141/o.: mauritius images/Maskot; S. 142/1 Zeilenweise v.l.n.r.: o.: Shutterstock.com/Preto Perola; S. 142/10: Shutterstock.com/VLADIMIR VK; S. 142/11,1: Shutterstock.com/RooftopStudioBangkok; S. 142/11,2: Shutterstock.com/Africa Studio; S. 142/12: Shutterstock.com/NJMSTOCK; S. 142/13 u.: stock.adobe.com/Dmitry Naumov; S. 142/14: Shutterstock.com/RooftopStudioBangkok; S. 142/15: Shutterstock.com/pornpawit; S. 142/16: Shutterstock.com/Sandratsky Dmitriy; S. 142/2: Shutterstock.com/Gemenacom; S. 142/3: Shutterstock.com/In Green; S. 142/4: Shutterstock.com/Jan Dix; S. 142/5 2.v.o.: Shutterstock.com/Anastasiia Horova; S. 142/6: Shutterstock.com/Nataliia K; S. 142/7: Shutterstock.com/Jag_cz; S. 142/8: stock.adobe.com/Kapawtord; S. 142/9 3.v.o.: Shutterstock.com/hidesy; S. 143/Emoji: Shutterstock.com/Yefym Turkin; S. 143/o.: stock.adobe.com/Maryna; S. 145/1 Zeilenweise v.l.n.r.: o.: Shutterstock.com/Focus and Blur; S. 145/10 u.: Shutterstock.com/Jukkis; S. 145/11: Shutterstock.com/BearFotos; S. 145/12: stock.adobe.com/JackF; S. 145/2: Shutterstock.com/wavebreakmedia; S. 145/3: Shutterstock.com/Monkey Business Images; S. 145/4 2.v.o.: Shutterstock.com/Kzenon; S. 145/5: stock.adobe.com/petunyia; S. 145/6: Shutterstock.com/videoTD; S. 145/7 3.v.o.: Shutterstock.com/VicVic Liu; S. 145/8: Shutterstock.com/Jacob Lund; S. 145/9: Shutterstock.com/PeopleImages.com - Yuri A; S. 146/bee: Shutterstock.com/Feng Lu; S. 146/butterfly: Shutterstock.com/CHAINFOTO24; S. 146/coast: stock.adobe.com/Gordon Fahey; S. 146/corn: Shutterstock.com/ABCDstock; S. 146/deer: Shutterstock.com/Radek Karko; S. 146/fox: Shutterstock.com/Sandra Standbridge; S. 146/frog: Shutterstock.com/Dinda Yulianto; S. 146/grass: Shutterstock.com/SHUTTER TOP; S. 146/mushroom: Shutterstock.com/romvo; S. 146/rocks: stock.adobe.com/pamela_d_mcadams; S. 146/valley: stock.adobe.com/Tomasz Zajda; S. 146/wave: stock.adobe.com/NorthShoreSurfPhotos; S. 147/m.l.: stock.adobe.com/M. Schoenfeld; S. 147/m.m.: stock.adobe.com/cceliaphoto; S. 147/m.r.: stock.adobe.com/Ralf; S. 147/o.l.: stock.adobe.com/motorradcbr; S. 147/o.m.: stock.adobe.com/Michael Conrad; S. 147/o.r.: stock.adobe.com/Sina Ettmer; S. 147/u.l.: stock.adobe.com/Leonid Andronov; S. 147/u.m.: stock.adobe.com/WernerHilpert; S. 147/u.r.: stock.adobe.com/M·H; S. 148/Ikons von: Shutterstock.com/Arafat Uddin; Shutterstock.com/Great_Kit; stock.adobe.com/anisa; stock.adobe.com/atScene; stock.adobe.com/Dilip; stock.adobe.com/iconin Ja; stock.adobe.com/KR Studio; stock.adobe.com/manstock007; stock.adobe.com/martialred; stock.adobe.com/North; stock.adobe.com/yoyonpujiono

**Textquellen**
S. 34: *All in this together: Zaina / https://www.museumoflondon.org.uk/discover/languages-london*

**Datenquellen**
S. 34: Die Karte basiert auf Daten (Census 2021) des Office for National Statistics in London, *https://www.ons.gov.uk/datasets/TS024/editions/2021/versions/1#version-history* (Zugriff: 16.08.2023); S. 112: Die statistischen Daten in Text A basieren auf Informationen von *https://cybercrew.uk/blog/cyberbullying-statistics-uk/* (Zugriff: 09.11.2023) und *https://www.mayoclinic.org/healthy-lifestyle/tween-and-teen-health/in-depth/teens-and-social-media-use/art-20474437#:~:text=Social%20media%20is%20a%20big,media%20 use%20have%20on%20 teens%3F* (Zugriff: 9.11.2023)